"There's nothing more to say."

Dawn continued packing as she spoke, moving from the closet to the suitcase, emptying one, filling the other.

"Except that we love each other." Michael was sitting on the bed, fully dressed, watching her.

Dawn glanced at Michael briefly. "We've gone over that, too."

"But when people are in love, they don't just write it off as a pleasant experience. They try to work things out. They live together, get married."

Dawn clutched a blouse to her breast. "In an ideal situation, people do those things. Ours is not ideal."

"So you're just going to fly back to Costa Rica and pretend I never existed?"

"You're wrong. I'll never forget you. I probably won't stop loving you, either. But if I had my choice, I *would* forget!"

Michael leaped from the bed and pulled her into his arms. Hurt, anger, passion were evident in the heat of his gaze. "I can't stop you from leaving," he said as his mouth claimed hers. "But I won't let you forget...."

Dear Reader,

It's a privilege to share with you the experience of writing Dawn and Michael's story. When these two characters first came to me, I wasn't sure how to accommodate them. Determined individuals, they insisted on creating their own, unprecedented, happy ending. Never mind what I, their frazzled creator, had to say!

Fortunately, my editors were sympathetic. They encouraged me to write the story, giving Dawn and Michael the latitude to make their relationship work. I was grateful and a little nervous. But in the process of writing, I was reminded that love can flourish only when we're accepted for who and what we are. Then the happy ending becomes the beginning.

Here's wishing all of you "Happy Beginnings!"
Elaine K. Stirling

Different Worlds

ELAINE K. STIRLING

Harlequin Books

TORONTO • NEW YORK • LONDON
AMSTERDAM • PARIS • SYDNEY • HAMBURG
STOCKHOLM • ATHENS • TOKYO • MILAN

To Ron,
my love, forever

Published January 1991

ISBN 0-373-25432-6

DIFFERENT WORLDS

1

MICHAEL C. GARRETT WAS, as usual, at the center of his universe. It was his first night in Costa Rica, and he faced a barrage of high-pressure meetings over the next few days. But impending challenges never bothered him. For now the beachside café was cool, the night breeze salty and his steak was done just right.

Then she walked in. A woman in tank top and shorts. Her shoulder-length brown hair was tied at the nape. Michael didn't quite catch the face. He had been too busy staring at her long, slim legs as she moved with confidence to the nearest bar stool.

Michael lay down his knife and fork. He watched her fluid gestures, listened to her laughter. Although he couldn't comprehend the words, he was struck by the elegant cadence of the woman's Spanish.

Something, and he didn't know what, shifted inside him. It was as though Michael C. Garrett was no longer at the center of his universe, but at the periphery of hers.

"HOLA, LITO. ¿CÓMO ESTÁ?" Dawn Avery leaned across the counter to kiss the burly bartender.

"Bien, chica. ¿Y tú?"

"Estupenda, gracias."

"This is a surprise, seeing you. When did you arrive in Puntarenas?"

"I just got off the train from San José. And you'll never believe it. We've acquired another hundred hectares for Montecristo. Isn't that wonderful?"

"Yes, it is wonderful. On whom did you work your charm this time?"

"The Bank of Hong Kong. Not bad, huh?"

Lito laughed. "No one but you could have won such a victory. If you keep this up, our entire nation will one day revert to rain forests."

"There's not much danger of that, Lito, but it's something to aspire to."

"Shall I prepare the usual, *chica?*"

"Please, I'm parched." She watched her friend fill a tall glass with crushed ice, club soda and a slice of lime. "Has Marisa had her baby yet?"

"No, poor thing, and she's five days overdue."

"Oh, dear, she must be so uncomfortable. How is Enrique handling it?"

Lito set the drink down with more force than necessary. "That useless son-in-law of mine. Marisa says he goes out every night and doesn't care at all about her condition."

"I'm sure Enrique cares," Dawn said, if only to make Lito feel better. "He's probably just nervous about the baby and doesn't know how to express his feelings."

"Hah, that's true enough. His only means of expression hangs between his legs."

Dawn laughed. "I guess we have ample proof of that."

Just then one of the bow-tied waiters appeared at her side. "*Perdone, chica,* but one of the customers would like to buy you a drink."

"Good grief," she muttered. "I just got here."

"You've broken your record," Lito said with a chuckle. "They usually wait at least five or ten minutes."

"But I only come here to see you. Why do your male customers always get the wrong idea?"

"Look at you, *chica*. How can they help it?"

Dawn brushed aside his praise. She wasn't unaware of her attractiveness, but she also appreciated the seductive ambience of Puntarenas. A sleepy town on Costa Rica's west coast, the port was a mecca for sailors, tourists, misfits and lonely hearts.

"If you owned a bakeshop, Lito, I wouldn't have this problem."

"If I owned a bakeshop, you would have no excitement in your life. Remember the invitation from the Argentine sea captain last month?"

"How could I forget? A two-week cruise to Los Angeles, all expenses paid, accompanied by forty-seven sailors. Excitement like that I can do without."

"So will you accept the offer of a drink?" the waiter asked.

"Please thank him, but no."

"Very well."

When the waiter left, Dawn struggled against an urge to peek at her latest Lothario. If the man couldn't come up with something more original than a drink, why should she care what he looked like? She should have known Lito would fill her in.

"A gringo. Looks rich, too."

"That's nice."

Dawn recalled with a shudder the last rich gringo who'd approached her at Lito's. He was an oil magnate from Texas who weighed about three hundred pounds and wheezed.

"If you treat him nicely," Lito suggested, "you might be able to secure another hundred hectares for your rain forest."

"You said the same thing about the Texan. The only thing he wanted to invest in was me."

"I can tell him to leave you alone."

"No, that's okay. If he comes around, I can handle it." Curiosity finally got the better of her, and Dawn turned. "Oh, shoot," she muttered, cursing her timing. The gringo caught her eye and lifted his beer in greeting. The waiter obviously hadn't relayed her message yet.

He was wearing a white shirt and gray pinstripes, obviously a corporate crusader of some kind. Talk about out of his element. This was the tropics, for heaven's sake! There wasn't a corporation for miles around.

Too late, Dawn realized he must have misinterpreted her curiosity. The man smiled and got up, bridging the distance between them in a few steps. She had no chance to escape.

"*Buenas noches,*" he said with a distinct gringo twang.

"*Buenas noches.*"

"Do you speak English?"

"Moderately well."

To Dawn's amusement the stranger's complexion deepened. "You're American?"

"According to my birth certificate, yes."

"Didn't mean to offend you, I just assumed...I mean, well, you look like a native."

"You didn't offend me. In fact, I take it as a compliment."

His expression eased. "It was meant as one."

If one could overlook his taste in beachwear, the man was attractive enough. His face was more interesting than handsome, with the crags and planes of a man over forty. He was tall, well built with thinning sandy hair and gentle blue-gray eyes . . . bedroom eyes. Inwardly Dawn laughed at the image. The guy probably kept a fax machine by his pillow.

When she'd finished her assessment, Dawn realized that his gaze, too, had slid downward. He seemed to have lost interest in the conversation. She should have said something quick and witty instead of letting the silence drag on. Dawn wrapped her legs around the bar stool, suddenly conscious of too much bare thigh.

Finally she conjured something to say. "You must be Canadian."

He looked up from her thighs. "How do you know?"

"The maple leaf. It'll give you away every time."

His glance fell again, but this time to his lapel. "I always wear this when I'm traveling."

"Why?"

"So people will know I'm, well—" he grinned sheepishly "—not American."

"No need to protect yourself in this country," she said, a trifle smug. "Costa Ricans love Americans."

"Oh, I see." With a deft motion he removed the pin and dropped it into his pocket. "Is that better?"

Dawn couldn't help laughing at his quick recovery. "You do catch on fast."

Just then the waiter hurried over, apologizing to Dawn in Spanish. Before she could reply he had turned to the Canadian. "I am sorry, *señor*. The lady does not wish to—"

"It's okay, Rafael," Dawn interjected.

"But you said—"

"I changed my mind. He can stay."

The waiter hovered, uncertain, then backed away. "*Muy bien, chica.*"

The Canadian watched him leave. "I didn't realize you had refused my offer."

"I had."

"But when you turned around . . ."

Dawn fibbed, none too convincingly. "I was trying to loosen a kink in my neck."

He gave her a look that was almost wounded, then just as quickly disarmed her with a grin. "My mistake. I've been known to make them."

His touch of shyness was charming. Then again, maybe it was an act. Either way it wouldn't hurt for Dawn to be sociable. The man probably didn't know a soul in Puntarenas.

And Lito could be right. With a little luck she might even talk this gringo into a worthwhile investment. He looked as though he could use a tax shelter or two.

"So you definitely won't let me buy you a drink," he said.

Dawn raised her club soda. "As you can see, I already have one."

"So you have. But could I join you, anyway?"

Lito, all two hundred pounds of him, leaned across the counter. Right on cue. Dawn surmised that the Canadian weighed about the same, but at well over six feet his weight was more effectively—and attractively—distributed.

The two men stared at each other in a classic male standoff, but the stranger stood his ground. Dawn couldn't help but be impressed. Usually Lito's tattoos were enough to keep predators at bay.

"It's okay," she said to Lito, then gestured to her new acquaintance. "Have a seat."

"Thanks." He eased himself onto the stool beside her. "Have you had dinner?"

"Just because I turned down a drink doesn't mean I was holding out for something better."

"I didn't think you were. I was just trying to regain my credibility."

"Assuming you had it in the first place."

When he hesitated, Dawn realized she might be coming down a little too defensively. Old habits, she told herself, pushing aside the soda. "Guess I could have something stronger. It's been a long day."

His look of relief touched a chord inside her. Smiling, he held out his hand. "Let's do it properly this time. I'm Michael Garrett from Winnipeg, Canada. How do you do?"

"Dawn Avery. Pleased to meet you." She liked the man's handshake. It was firm, assertive.

"What part of the States are you from?" he asked.

"I was born in Oregon, but Dad was in the army, so we moved around a lot."

"A citizen of the world, are you?"

"I've never thought of it that way. Home is just wherever I happen to be at the time."

"Sounds like a healthy attitude. So tell me, what does a citizen of the world like to drink?"

Dawn thought for a moment. "Campari and soda." It was the most cosmopolitan drink she could think of—and one that was usually beyond her means.

Michael motioned to Lito. "Campari and soda for the lady, please. And I'll have another beer."

The bartender was already preparing her drink, making it patently evident he'd been eavesdropping. But if Michael noticed, he didn't seem to mind. He turned, planted an elbow on the bar and studied Dawn.

His scrutiny was enough to make her squirm. "You're not going to ask the obvious question, are you?" she said.

"Which is?"

"What's a nice girl like me—"

"Doing in a place like this? I intended to, but you probably wouldn't give me a straight answer, anyway."

"How do you know?"

"Call it a hunch." Michael took a sip of his beer.

She felt her cheeks turn a little pink.

"Come to think of it," he said, as though to restore her confidence, "people do use stupid clichés when they meet in a bar."

Dawn laughed. "I'll say. In this bar I've heard them in twenty-five languages."

"Multilingual, too, are you?"

At first she didn't catch the implication. But this time he didn't make her feel embarrassed. "Guess I had that one coming to me."

Dawn liked Michael's subtle wit, the boyish glint in his eyes. The beachside ambience seemed to be loosening him up. If only he would do the same with his tie.

"So, do you come here often?" Michael groaned and covered his face. "I can't believe I said that."

"Neither can I. But just to clear up the issue, I don't come in here to pick up men. The bartender happens to be an old friend."

"I believe you," he insisted.

His expression, more than his words, convinced Dawn that he did. "What's your excuse?" she asked, recrossing her legs.

"For being in a bar?"

"For being in Costa Rica."

"I'm here on business."

"I never would have guessed." Dawn gave him what should have been a harmless once-over, but she didn't quite manage. At a few strategic spots her gaze lingered. Shoulders, thighs, the subtle rise of fabric at his groin.

Not that Dawn could see anything through the Savile Row wool. Not that she wanted to.

"Seriously, though." She cleared her throat for emphasis. "Puntarenas is hardly a corporate nerve center. Did you take a wrong turn somewhere?"

"I'm just spending the night here. Tomorrow I head for Guanacaste to visit a client's subsidiary."

"What kind of subsidiary?"

"They're a feed and grain company."

"Oh."

"Do you have something against feed and grain?"

She curled her fingers around the drink. "What makes you say that?"

"Come on, if you had dropped that 'oh' from a second-story window, you might have killed someone."

She had to give him silent credit for perception. "I have nothing against feed and grain. It just depends on what's being fed and why."

"Most of it goes to beef cattle."

"That's what I figured." So much for appealing to Michael's philanthropy. Not only would he have little interest in the Montecristo rain forest, they would do well to emerge from this discussion on speaking terms.

"I've obviously hit a nerve," he said. "Are you a vegetarian or something?"

"Good grief, no."

"Then what exactly is your stance?"

Wrinkling her brow, Dawn tried to ignore the crags in Michael's face and the fullness of his lower lip. She ought to be excited about educating a member of the North American corporate class. This was a rare opportunity. That Michael Garrett was attractive and fascinating was beside the point.

"Did you know," she said, "that seventy percent of Costa Rica's farmland is in pasture for beef cattle?"

"Yes."

"And do you know where most of that beef goes?"

"Tell me," he said with the steady look of someone who already had the answer.

"It's shipped to North America where it ends up in greasy fast-food hamburgers."

"That makes Costa Rican beef a viable export, wouldn't you say?"

"Sure. An export that's destroying the domestic environment, not to mention the world's."

Michael leaned forward. His gaze rested briefly on her mouth, then lifted to her eyes. "This is probably a stupid question, but what do you do for a living?"

She squared her shoulders proudly. "I'm a biologist at the Montecristo rain forest."

"Boy, do I know how to pick them," he replied with a laugh. When Dawn didn't laugh in return, he took another sip of his drink. After a minute or so, he said, "Well?"

"Well, what?"

"Aren't you going to enlighten me on the sins of soil erosion and deforestation?"

Dawn's eyes widened. She prided herself on being well informed. Being predictable was not nearly as satisfying. "You mean you're familiar with Costa Rica's ecological problems?"

"I do my homework."

"Then you understand my position."

"Completely."

Dawn folded her arms. "So aren't you even going to defend yours?"

"Nope."

"Why not?"

"Because I came here to enjoy my dinner—and with a little luck, your company. I don't enjoy talking shop unless I absolutely have to."

He might have been patronizing her. Dawn wasn't sure. If he was, she had reason to take offense. She had waged dozens of environmental battles, and though the odds were stacked against her, she sometimes made headway. There was no reason to wish that the subject, this time, had never come up.

Michael reached over and touched her hand. "Believe it or not, I do understand your position."

His touch sent a tremor along her arm, a tremor that Dawn refused to entertain. "Lip service, Mr. Garrett, isn't going to save the world's rain forests."

"Neither is one voice crying in the wilderness—or in this case, a Costa Rican bar."

"Change has to begin somewhere, even if it means changing one mind at a time."

"Assuming we're in opposition, which I don't think we are. And like I said, I don't feel like ruining our perfect evening."

Dawn's adrenaline had begun pumping madly. Maybe that explained her slightly breathless reply. "*Our* perfect evening?"

"That's right. I happen to love this planet, too, and maybe one day I'll tell you what I'm doing to help. But not tonight, not when there's a sky full of stars just begging to be noticed."

Damn it, she realized now she could have won this debate. The statistics were all in her favor. But something inside Dawn melted. Something inside her beckoned to those same neglected stars.

"How long are you going to be in Costa Rica?" she asked cautiously.

"Until the end of the week."

"Would you have time to visit Montecristo?"

"I could make the time."

"You're not just saying that to appease me?"

"Are you kidding?" He flashed another irresistible grin. "That's exactly why I'm saying it."

Dawn let out a long breath, feeling as though she'd narrowly averted disaster, one both needless and irreparable. If she handled things properly, even his somewhat childish wit, Michael Garrett might prove to be a valuable contact. If she didn't, this opportunity would be lost forever, and all she'd have left was her pride.

"All right," Dawn said, "we'll postpone this discussion until you've seen Montecristo."

MICHAEL REALIZED he could have won this debate. The statistics were all in his favor. But one look into Dawn's eyes was enough to quash the urge. They were lovely eyes, green and flecked with gold. The color of sincerity, he thought, if sincerity had a color. Also keenly intelligent, they'd begun to smolder at his last idiotic remark.

A man would be foolish to cross Dawn Avery unprepared. And Michael, who was far from foolish, had almost done that very thing.

"Are we really calling a truce?" he asked, treading lightly.

"We can if you'd like."

"I'd like." The sense of relief that flooded through him was unnerving. As though he actually needed this woman's respect. "So tell me, how well do you know Puntarenas?"

"Like the back of my hand."

Dawn had flinched the last time he touched her, but mostly, he suspected, out of surprise. Her arm was now resting on the bar, her fingers flexed. Michael moved more slowly this time, making sure she had time to react. He took her hand. She didn't pull away, and that pleased him. Gently he traced her veins and tendons with his fingertip. *Here goes nothing...*

"This is my first night in Puntarenas, Dawn, and I don't know a soul. Would you care to show me around?"

DAWN UNZIPPED her travel bag and dumped the contents onto the bed. Everything, as usual, was wrinkled. She was such a rotten packer, and there wasn't time to ask the desk clerk for an iron.

Michael was going to meet her in the lobby in fifteen minutes. It was hardly a coincidence that they were staying in the same hotel. The Tioga was the best place in town, and by North American standards a bargain—even for impoverished biologists.

Her one decent outfit would have to suffice. Dawn had bought the skirt in Peru several years ago. Made of black cotton, it featured an inset of black lace extending from midthigh to knees. The blouse was red silk and sleeveless with a slightly draped neckline. At least she'd had the sense to pack the blouse with reasonable care.

Impressing men with her fashion sense was hardly Dawn's style. But in Michael's case it was more like meeting him halfway. He had volunteered to change into something more casual, and somehow Dawn doubted that anything in his wardrobe would complement her tank top and baggy shorts.

She undid her ponytail and brushed her hair vigorously, pleased with the thick curls that tumbled across her shoulders. Long hair was Dawn's only indulgence in a profession that favored something short and simple. As for makeup, she seldom bothered. Living in Costa Rica gave her a year-round tan, and the humidity of Montecristo kept her skin reasonably youthful.

If Michael was looking for glamour, he'd come to the wrong lady. But she doubted that he suffered such illusions. Besides, something had obviously compelled him to buy her a drink, and for that Dawn was grateful. It had been a long time since she'd enjoyed the sheer pleasure of being a woman. And some feminine wisdom told her that being a woman in Michael Garrett's company could be sheer pleasure.

HE COULDN'T TAKE his eyes off her. She was descending the stairs while a breeze from the lobby billowed her skirt and pressed the red blouse gently to her breasts. Dawn's figure was graceful and willowy—what Michael would call femininity in moderation. At forty-two he had been around long enough to sample the extremes. And tonight extremes didn't appeal.

"You look gorgeous," he murmured.

"Thank you," she ventured with a smile. "You look pretty fine yourself."

Michael had shed his corporate weeds for a pair of light gray slacks and a pale blue shirt. Granted, the shirt was pin-striped, but the touch of formality suited him. Interestingly enough, so did his receding hairline. It gave him a refined, worldly appearance, like that of a man who'd worked with diligence to get where he was.

"Where would you like to go first?" Dawn asked.

"How about someplace where we could dance?"

A shiver of delight raced along her spine. "I was hoping you might say that."

They crossed the street to the walkway along the beach. For a while neither spoke, and that was okay. Dawn was happy to listen to the waves and subtle, inner murmurs of anticipation.

She seldom indulged herself anymore in the pleasures of meeting men. There was always so much work, and so little time. No, Dawn corrected herself sharply. She could have made the time for men, but those who crossed her path were either forgettable or embroiled in some hopeless emotional crisis. Neither type, she had learned, was worth the bother.

"This place seems interesting," Michael said, pointing to a nightclub overlooking the water.

"I was about to suggest this place myself."

It occurred to her that tonight could be just another exercise in futility. But futility was always preceded by expectations, and Dawn wasn't expecting anything. At thirty-five she had finally discovered how to be happy with herself. Therefore, an evening with an attractive man was a bonus—not cause for self-pity.

The nightclub was a favorite among locals. Taped salsa music rocked the crowded dance floor, rendering conversation impossible and redundant. Entering the cavernous room, Dawn decided to abandon inhibitions and slip her hand into Michael's. After all, she rationalized, it was the only way to penetrate the crowd without losing each other.

They found a small corner table and ordered drinks while the atmosphere worked its magic. Like most places in town, the nightclub was open-air, wafting Latin rhythms across the Gulf of Nicoya and receiving fresh sea air in return.

Dawn sensed a similar exchange between her and Michael. A combination of curiosity, sexual attraction and a mutual desire to make the evening special. There were a thousand questions Dawn wanted to ask, a thousand things she'd have liked to say. But words would have been lost in the music, both cluttering and complicating. For now it was enough simply to enjoy.

"Let's dance," Michael said, reaching his hand across the table.

"Yes, let's."

The pulse of the music was fast, which made no difference to the couples on the dance floor. It was too crowded to dance properly, anyway. The music was an excuse to touch, a reason for bodies to explore and sample.

Michael, who had obviously assessed the situation, opened his arms to Dawn. She stepped into his embrace, closed her eyes and abandoned herself to pure sensation.

He was tall enough that she could rest her head comfortably on his chest. His cotton shirt was thin, and Dawn could feel the dense hair on his chest. Breathing deeply, she reveled in the scent of his soap and his body. If a woman was the least bit vulnerable—unlike Dawn—she could burrow into this man's arms and never want to surface.

Effortlessly the two of them captured the rhythm. The fit of their bodies was astonishing. Hips and legs seemed to know precisely where to touch, how to arouse. Never had Dawn been more aware of dance as sexual play. Yet the realization wasn't disturbing. Michael's movements were neither manipulative nor aggressive. He was merely responding, as was she, to the natural impulse of their bodies.

The Spanish lyrics echoed the passion. *Te quiero, te quiero. Ay, que te quiero* ... Dawn had always been intrigued by the Spanish phrase for *I love you*. Literally translated it meant "I want you." Such an uncomplicated, honest admission—unlike the three dreaded words in English.

Feeling reckless, Dawn mouthed the phrase *"Te quiero"* against Michael's chest. He couldn't possibly have seen or heard her, yet his response was electric. He shuddered, paused briefly, then tightened his embrace.

A new song began, but neither of them pulled away. Instead, Michael tangled his fingers in Dawn's hair and drew her head back. Their gazes locked, and for a long while they danced in each other's eyes. Then he pressed his mouth to her forehead.

Dawn's pulse, already racing, quickened even more. His lips on her skin was not so much a kiss as a sweet, silent invasion. It was only her forehead, yet something inside her seemed to flower, open up, invite.

"Oh, Michael," she moaned, moving her hips against his.

Then she felt a wallop on her shoulder. *"¡Hola, chica!"*

Dawn pulled herself from Michael's arms and turned to find Lito's son-in-law, Enrique, grinning idiotically. His arm was draped around some young thing, and the two of them were swaying—but not to the music. Enrique was as drunk as a skunk.

2

"ENRIQUE, WHAT ARE YOU doing here?" Dawn demanded.

"Having a good time, jus' like you."

"You ought to be at home with Marisa. Why, she could be in labor this very minute." But her words were lost in a pounding conga rhythm. Enrique had no idea he was being scolded. Or if he did, he just didn't care.

"Wanna dance, *chica?*" The young man winked and wiggled his hips.

Dawn clenched her teeth. "No, thank you. As you can see, I already have a partner." A partner, she noticed, who was sharing her irritation. "Michael, this is Enrique. Enrique, Michael."

Michael held out his hand for a perfunctory shake, but the young man's attention was already elsewhere. He was slobbering kisses on his miniskirted companion.

"Why that no-good, two-timing . . ." Dawn muttered.

But Michael, unaware of the situation, couldn't have understood. He lowered his head to her ear. "Could we get back to what we were doing?"

His breath tickled sensitive places along her scalp. His nuzzled request evoked an even deeper response. Dawn would have loved to resume her exploration of Michael's body. But Enrique and her sense of ethics wouldn't let her.

"I can't." She rose on tiptoe to speak into his ear. Her cheek rasped against new stubble, a sensation Dawn tried to disregard. "Enrique's wife is a friend of mine, and she's nine months pregnant."

Michael drew his head back slowly, enhancing the erotic friction. Then he looked over his shoulder. "She doesn't look pregnant."

"That's not his wife."

"Oh. So what are you planning to do?"

He was talking to Dawn face-to-face, so close they could have kissed. And judging from his expression, their thoughts were dallying along the same lines. But one glance at Enrique reminded Dawn there was enough ill-placed dallying going on. "I have to find a way to get Enrique home."

The two of them turned to find Enrique rubbing his pelvis against the woman's miniskirt. She was pursing her lips and mussing his hair. The music was too loud to hear her cooing.

"Unless you're Enrique's mother," Michael said, "getting him home could be tricky."

"I know."

"So how do you propose to convince him?"

"Forcibly, if necessary." Dawn clamped her hands on the young man's shoulders and yanked hard, nearly toppling the couple.

"Hey, what you doin'?" he said, stumbling backward against Dawn.

"I'm taking you home," she growled in his ear.

"I don't wanna go."

With a murderous glare the young woman yanked him back into her clutches. "You hear Rique? He doesn't wanna go."

"Too bad. He's going, anyway," Dawn replied in Spanish, extracting him again.

"Why should I?" Yank. "I found him first."

"That's what you think, sweetie."

The human tug-of-war might have continued indefinitely if Michael hadn't stepped forward. "Looks like you could use some interference."

Dawn looked up with relief. "You're right. I could."

She was expecting Michael to lend his muscles, the very ones she'd been feeling up so enjoyably a few minutes ago. Instead, he sidled up to Enrique's date. "Hello, what's your name?"

The woman looked up suspiciously. Then she looked again and, apparently liking what she saw, smiled and batted her fake lashes. *"No hablo inglés, señor."*

Michael scratched his chin. "Uh, let's see, then. *Cómo te*, uh . . . *cómo se—*"

"Her name ish Carmen," Enrique slurred, "but you stay away from her. She is my wo-man."

"Sure, whatever you say." Michael gave him an indulgent nod, then wrapped an arm around Carmen's shoulders. "So, Carmen, why don't we all go into the lobby where we can talk?"

She couldn't understand a word, but Michael had the earmarks of a rich gringo. That was reason enough, Dawn surmised, for Carmen to agree to anything.

His suave approach worked. Carmen duly followed Michael, Enrique lathered after Carmen and Dawn brought up the rear. As soon as they reached the brightly lit lobby, Enrique clutched his stomach and doubled over. "I'm gonna be sick."

"Oh, great," Dawn muttered.

"I'll take care of him." Michael hoisted the young man to a semivertical stance and hauled him to the men's room.

Carmen and Dawn waited in the lobby, female static crackling between them. "You know he's married, don't you?" Dawn remarked.

"You mean the gringo?"

Dawn opened her mouth, then closed it again. She had no idea whether Michael was married or not. If he was, she had a lot of nerve lecturing Carmen. Except, as Dawn reminded herself smugly, she and Michael had only danced. They hadn't actually necked or pawed each other with the express intention of—

"So tell me," Carmen demanded. "Which one's married?"

"Enrique," Dawn replied, not sounding quite so sanctimonious. Her intentions with Michael were still a little blurry, but she preferred to leave them unexamined for now.

"Rique never told me he had a wife."

"He does, and she's going to have a baby any minute—their eleventh."

The white lie, totally unpremeditated, was for Marisa's sake. Women who looked like Carmen were seldom intimidated by the existence of a spouse. In fact, they took it as a challenge. But Carmen was obviously not bright enough to realize Enrique was too young to have that many kids. Her eyes widened in horror. "Eleven. *¡Madre de Dios!*"

"That's right. He just loves babies. It's the only reason he likes women."

"He's not going to turn me into no baby machine."

"Can't say I blame you."

With a swivel of her pencil-thin hips, Carmen sashayed back into the dance hall. In her wake surged a crowd of single men. Carmen wouldn't be alone for long.

"So much for her," Dawn muttered, returning her attention to the men's room entrance. After a minute or two, Michael emerged with a pale, shaky Enrique in tow.

"This guy's in bad shape," Michael said. "There's no way he can drive."

"It wouldn't matter. He doesn't own a car."

"Where does he live?"

"A few blocks from here."

"Then we could put him in a cab," Michael said. *And forget all about him*, said his hopeful expression.

A part of Dawn agreed. She would have just as soon packed him in a crate heading downstream. "It's hard to find a cab at this time of night, and I'd like to make sure he gets home okay. Marisa, his wife, must be frantic by now."

"Are you thinking of walking him home?"

It wasn't like Dawn to hesitate when it came to helping a friend. Enrique wasn't her friend, but Marisa was. In some ways she was like a baby sister to Dawn. "It's probably the best way. The fresh air will do him good. But you don't have to come with me."

"I know, but I think you could use some help, and I don't have other plans."

She could understand Michael's lack of enthusiasm. Ten minutes ago they'd been sharing something special. Now they were playing nursemaid to a drunk. But at least he had agreed to come along. With a little luck they might still salvage something from the evening.

"Thank you," she said with a look of gratitude.

When they escorted the father-to-be outdoors, the fresh air induced another case of heaves. This time Michael pointed him in the direction of the nearest hedge and waited a safe distance away with Dawn.

"He seems awfully young to have a pregnant wife."

"He's nineteen," Dawn replied. "Marisa's all of seventeen."

Michael shook his head. "There ought to be a law against getting married before thirty."

"Speaking from experience?" Dawn asked, trying to sound disinterested.

"I'll say. I got married at twenty and didn't know the first thing about commitment."

"And now?" she said, holding her breath.

"Now I'm forty-two, divorced and still not too sure about that three-syllable word."

Dawn laughed. "Commitment? I think it has something to do with mental institutions."

Just then Enrique staggered out of the bushes and glanced around blearily. He must have forgotten how he'd gotten there. He was about to return indoors when Michael stopped him. "Oh, no, you don't. We're going this way."

Still confused, Enrique tried to execute a punch, but his aim was off, and the effort nearly knocked him over. Dawn ran to Michael's rescue, grabbing the young man's free arm. Enrique weighed a ton. So much for small talk on this journey.

Twenty minutes later, sweating and exhausted from supporting Enrique between them, Michael and Dawn came to a tiny concrete-block home. "We're here," Dawn said.

She looked about as fed up as Michael felt. But he was glad he hadn't let Dawn do this on her own. Part of him had responded out of chivalry, but another part didn't want to let her disappear into the night. Not yet, when things were just beginning.

Dawn was about to knock when the door swung open. A young woman appeared, a dented frying pan poised above her head. Michael couldn't understand the barrage of Spanish directed at Enrique, but instinct told him this wasn't a friendly greeting.

Then Dawn said something to the woman. Woman, hell, Michael thought, amending his opinion. Despite her advanced pregnancy, Enrique's wife was little more than a child herself.

"Marisa Valenzuela, this is Michael Garrett," Dawn said, switching to English. "He helped me bring Enrique home."

"Hello," Marisa said, turning huge, fearful eyes in his direction.

Michael took her hand. "Sorry to disturb you so late."

She shrugged. "No problem. I was awake."

Marisa's show of courage was unconvincing. Her pretty face was taut with fear.

"You haven't gone into labor or anything?" Dawn asked.

"No, the baby is not ready." Marisa stepped aside so that Dawn and Michael could bring her husband inside.

"Which way is the bedroom?" Michael asked.

"Not the bedroom, please!" Marisa clutched her abdomen and dropped her gaze, embarrassed. "If he wakes up, he will only want to . . ."

"Okay." Michael clenched his teeth. "We'll put him on the sofa." He would just as soon have punched the creep, but Enrique was out cold and wouldn't have appreciated the message.

Wordlessly Marisa watched them lay him down. Then she disappeared for a minute and returned with a tattered blanket that she placed over her husband.

Something about the gesture made Michael's eyes sting, and he had to look away. Maybe it was Marisa's capacity to forgive. Or maybe he was feeling a twinge of envy. Enrique didn't deserve the love of a good woman, but the love was there. It wasn't a question Michael had ever pondered before, but where was the justice?

He looked up at Dawn and saw the same telltale shine in her eyes. But it had to be a coincidence. They couldn't possibly be thinking the same thing.

Their gazes held, intense and inquiring. Then Dawn pulled away as though she'd allowed Michael to see too much. Or maybe he was the one who'd done the revealing.

"Would you like some tea or coffee?" Dawn asked Marisa.

"No, thank you. I am going to bed soon."

"But what if the baby comes tonight? Enrique won't be any help."

"Our neighbors have a car. They have promised to take me to the hospital."

"That's good to hear." Dawn glanced around the room with the look of someone who wanted to help but knew she couldn't. "Well, guess we'll be off then. I'll be at the Tioga tonight if you need anything."

"Thank you, both of you."

"You're welcome," Michael said, touching her shoulder lightly.

Marisa walked them to the door. "Dawn?" she said in a small voice.

When Dawn's shoulders tensed, Michael felt a respondent pull within himself. He'd always been perceptive, quick to pick up on other people's signals. He knew what Marisa was about to ask; the reply, for Dawn, wouldn't be easy.

"Yes, Marisa?"

"Was Rique . . . was he with another woman tonight?"

The room grew prickly with silence as the two women looked at each other. *Don't tell her*, Michael urged silently. Not tonight. The truth would hurt her more than she's already hurting.

"No, Marisa," Dawn replied. "As far as I know, Enrique was just drinking tonight."

"YOU DID THE RIGHT THING, you know, not telling Marisa," Michael said when they were alone on the street.

"I'm not so sure it was the right thing. If Enrique is running around—which he obviously is—his wife has the right to know."

"But not when she's about to give birth."

Street lamps had cast Michael's face in shadow, but Dawn could read the compassion in his eyes. "You're right," she said at last. "Marisa doesn't need more problems right now."

"Neither do we," he said, slipping an arm around her waist.

It was precisely what Dawn had hoped he would do. She needed to be touched, to be reconnected with happy feelings. Why Michael should be the one to make that happen was probably nothing more than circumstance, just as leaning against him made it easier to walk in step. There was no need to read more into the situation.

"I really appreciate your helping me out," Dawn said.

"My pleasure," he answered, as though it really was.

She looked away, apprehensive of this sudden onrush of feelings. Gratitude, she could understand. Michael had earned that by accompanying her tonight. But these other emotions were not to be trusted. They were illusive, conjured things, swirling and dancing at the edges of her mind. No matter what happened, she was certain that, by morning, they'd be gone.

"What would you like to do now?" Michael asked.

Dawn thought a moment. Dancing no longer appealed to her. There were too many people. And after witnessing Enrique's performance, she didn't care for more alcohol. "How about we just walk along the beach?"

"Sounds perfect."

They turned off the residential street onto the main boulevard of Puntarenas. The beach was a block away, but Dawn could already hear the waves, feel the sting of salt on her face.

"How long have you known Marisa?" Michael asked.

"Since she was little."

"I thought you two seemed close."

"We are. When I was in high school, I lived with her family as an exchange student. Lito, the bartender, is her father."

"That explains a few things."

Dawn smiled, mellowed by reminiscence. "I remember Marisa's fondest dream was to work in a dress shop in San José. Then she met Enrique, and three months later she was pregnant."

"Is that the only reason she married him?"

"In this part of the world it's reason enough." Although she cared deeply, thinking about Marisa was distressing. And right now Dawn wanted nothing to do with distress. There had been enough intrusions. "I didn't give you much of a tour tonight."

"Yes, you did. You showed me all kinds of things— mostly about yourself."

Dawn's steps slowed, then stopped altogether. "What do you mean?" she asked, turning to him.

"You've shown me your humor, your style and how attractive you are. You've also shown me that you're a good person."

The night breeze was rippling Michael's shirt, outlining the strong contours of his body. When, Dawn wondered, had he undone the top three buttons? When had he changed from a stuffy corporate knight to a living, breathing man? Or was it she who, until now, had failed to notice?

"I didn't realize that I was part of tonight's itinerary," she said softly.

"You were. I really wasn't that interested in seeing Puntarenas." He took her hands and stroked her palms with his thumbs. "Something happened to us back there on the dance floor, Dawn."

"Sure, Enrique nearly threw up on us."

Even before Michael flinched she regretted her glibness. Dawn had been pondering those few precious minutes herself ever since they'd left the nightclub. They had danced together, and danced beautifully. Words like enchantment and magic kept creeping into her mind. But sappy romanticism wasn't part of Dawn's vocabulary—or her reality.

"It was special," she managed to admit, "but I don't know how to put it into words."

"Neither do I, but it was like an...energy between us."

Dawn smiled. Yes, energy. She had felt it herself, acknowledged the exchange without questioning the source. Yet she was, by nature, an analyst. If there was a reasonable explanation—and there had to be—for the chemistry between her and Michael, she would find it.

"Costa Rica's a sensuous country," she ventured. "The music, the people—everyone falls under its spell sooner or later."

"Is that what you think happened tonight?"

"Maybe." It couldn't have been disappointment she was seeing in his eyes. Surely his ego wasn't that fragile.

"What about you, Dawn? Have you ever fallen under Costa Rica's spell?"

"Are you kidding? I've been spellbound by this place for years. That's why I promised myself I'd live here one day."

"So you think it was just the atmosphere that made our dancing special."

She could have lied, protected him from the truth as she'd done with Marisa tonight. But honesty had always been Dawn's greatest strength—at other times, her weakness. "No, I'm not saying that at all. Whatever was happening between us, I wish it could have continued."

Michael's eyes brightened. "So do I."

They resumed their stroll, arm in arm, to the beach. A crescent moon hung low over the Gulf of Nicoya. Along the horizon lights from an anchored freighter were strung like silver beads against obsidian. They found a bench with a perfect view and sat down.

"Are you involved with anyone?" Michael asked.

The urge to say yes was ridiculous. There was no one in Dawn's life at the moment, except Michael. And no matter how enchanting the evening, a person didn't become "involved" in a matter of hours. And so she hedged once again. "Do you think I'd have gone out with you if I was?"

Michael studied her for a while, as though not quite trusting her reply. "I guess that would depend on your relationship."

"Well, I'm not involved, thank heavens." Her attempt to sound independent wasn't as convincing as usual. But Michael didn't know her, so maybe he wouldn't notice.

"A free spirit, are you?"

"Nothing that glamorous," she said. "I'm just a work-aholic scientist."

"Even workaholics find time to fall in love."

Dawn shook her head emphatically. "Not this one. I know it sounds hokey, but I really do love my work. I can't imagine one person affecting me so strongly that I'd want to give up my career."

"Why would you have to do that?"

"I live in the middle of a jungle, and I never know for how long. I could be in Costa Rica one year, Brazil the next. Then there are symposiums, visiting professor-ships. Just try and find a man who would accept all that traveling."

"I travel all the time."

"But don't you see? It's different for men. They can expect their wives to wait patiently at home, or to pull up roots when it's time to move. I should know. Dad was in the army, and we moved fourteen times."

"Did your mother ever complain?"

"Mom complained all the time, but she still packed up and followed him. I'm afraid I'm not into martyrdom. And I wouldn't want a martyr for a husband, either."

"I can see how your odds are kind of narrowed."

Narrowed odds. The words stung far too much for Dawn's liking. But Michael wasn't telling her anything she didn't already know, or accept, about herself. "What about you?" she asked. "Did traveling contribute to your marriage breaking up?"

Michael laughed wryly. "It probably kept things going longer than they should have."

"What do you mean?"

"Looking back, I realize my wife and I never did com-municate, not even at the beginning. So traveling became a form of escape. As long as I was on the road, I didn't have to cope with problems at home."

"But eventually they caught up with you."

"Until you resolve them, problems always do."

"I know," Dawn admitted, much to her surprise. "I was married, too."

"You?" Michael said.

She laughed at his tone of disbelief. "He was a geologist. We met in college. After we were married we both landed jobs in Indonesia."

"Sounds ideal."

"It was, sort of, until my grant ran out. I accepted the nearest position I could find. It was in the Philippines. We tried the long-distance stuff for a while—visiting back and forth, spending a fortune on long-distance calls."

"I've never believed those relationships could work."

"Neither do I now. Without realizing, we'd developed different life-styles, different friends. The clincher came when I paid a surprise visit to my husband and found him in bed with one of his female associates." Dawn toyed with the lace on her skirt. The memory, she discovered, was no longer painful, just embarrassing. That she'd blurted it to Michael made no sense whatsoever.

"I'm sorry," Michael said.

"Thanks, but I never really blamed him. We were living apart even when we were together."

For a long while the two of them stared out to sea. Then Michael spoke again. "Do you ever get lonely being on your own?"

"Sometimes. Do you?"

"Yes."

"But despite the loneliness I've come to the conclusion that alone is definitely better."

Michael reached out and gently laid her head against his shoulder. "You know what, Dawn?"

"Mmm?" she said, snuggling closer.

"I've come to the same conclusion."

3

DAWN DIDN'T FEEL like talking anymore. With her hand splayed across his chest, she could feel Michael's heartbeat and the thick mat of hair, coiled and springy, against her fingers. The sensations were almost dizzying.

If Michael was aware of her reaction, he gave no notice. "Have you ever been tempted to remarry?" he asked.

"Never," she said with just the slightest flicker of hesitation.

"Me, neither," he replied, equally emphatic.

Maybe, on second thought, it wouldn't hurt to keep the conversation flowing. Otherwise she might be tempted to do something reckless like run her tongue along his collarbone.

"You must have plenty of opportunities to meet women," she said.

"Yes, but I've finally learned what most of them are after." Michael pressed his fingers into the tender indentations between Dawn's ribs. She nearly gasped.

"You can't blame them. You've got a great body."

He laughed. "I wasn't talking about sex."

"You weren't?"

His hand had stopped just below the swell of her breast—a precarious resting place, considering the nature of this discussion. "You don't know the corporate world like I do," he said. "What women want these days is money, prestige and a glamorous life-style. Sex is the commodity they use to get it."

Dawn must have been living in the jungle too long. She couldn't even imagine that kind of behavior. "Sounds vicious."

"It is."

"Doesn't love ever enter the picture?"

"I'm not sure I know the meaning of that word." He looked at her with a curious smile. "Do you?"

"I don't think so."

Michael tousled her hair. "Hey, stop looking so glum. This wasn't a quiz."

"You're right," she said, returning his smile.

"And just because we both like solitude doesn't mean we can't enjoy evenings like this."

"Right again." Despite her glib response, Dawn sensed a flaw in Michael's argument. Enjoying solitude was all the more reason to avoid evenings like this with their resultant complications. She opened her mouth, intending to clarify that point. But Michael kissed her before she had a chance.

As soon as his mouth touched hers, Dawn's philosophy lost ground. She could have pulled away, but the kiss was too heady. Words couldn't compete.

By wrapping her arms around his neck, she dared him to challenge her perception. If Michael truly believed that evenings like this were meant to be enjoyed, let him prove it with his body as well as his mind.

Instinctively he must have picked up on the challenge. Michael's kisses were neither gentle nor retiring. They were demanding, provocative. He probed her mouth with his tongue, as if seeking Dawn's vulnerable areas. And there were many, she was beginning to realize. Skimming her teeth, dallying with the tender flesh beneath her tongue, every kiss was a silent rebuttal to which she could only respond in kind.

When he sensed her compliance, Michael's passion intensified. His lips traveled her face, her chin and jaw-line. He nipped lightly at her earlobe. With his breath he fanned the small hairs at her nape.

"You're so beautiful," he whispered. "I can't be-lieve . . ."

Dawn felt rather than heard the words. The phrase needed no completion, nor could there be any argument. Her physical self understood, far better than she, the yearning that inspired his embrace.

She laced her fingers through his hair while her blouse pulled free of the skirt. Michael's hand was already at her waist. When he touched bare skin, she ignited even more.

Doubts flared up to tamp the passion. Dawn didn't want this to be a one-night tumble, a senseless free-fall to her younger days. But the night breeze, in some strange way, seemed to whisper reassurances. And although the beach was a public place, darkness had settled over them like a velvet cloak. There was no one to see, hear—or judge.

Michael's hand moved upward and found her breast. Dawn's nipples, already taut, hardened even more. She cupped his face and traced the whiskered contours of his neck. Her thumbs lingered in the hair that peeked above his collar.

Then their mouths came together again to silence whatever protests might still linger in Dawn's mind. And they were there, insidious, logical words of warning. *This man is a stranger, Dawn. Making love would be a mistake, and you don't make mistakes with men any-more.*

She rejected the words, pushed their truth away. Right now Dawn didn't want truth. She wanted only to feel. To reconfirm her womanhood, her capacity to entice.

Denial had no place in these caresses. Dawn knew only that she needed Michael. To what end, for what reason, was not yet an issue.

"You are magic," he whispered, fumbling with the constraints of her blouse.

"So are you," Dawn returned, arching back and gasping when he took a nipple in his mouth. "Oh, Michael . . ."

Words were lost, doubts quenched by the fluid response of her body. She stroked his forehead as he suckled. She pressed herself to him, wanting to please and intent on showing him just how much.

But instead of responding as she'd hoped, Michael drew back with a sigh. He returned her blouse to its rightful position. "We can't do this, Dawn. Not here."

Relief and confusion swirled through her mind as she rearranged her clothes. He was right, of course. "I don't know what to say, Michael. This isn't like me to . . ."

Gently he lifted her chin. "To what, Dawn? Want someone?"

"What I mean is, I don't usually do this kind of thing. Meet a man in a bar and . . . well, you know."

"I figured that much out in the first ten minutes."

"But it didn't stop you from trying."

"The last time I picked up a woman in a bar, they were still calling them discos."

Dawn laughed in spite of herself. "Get out, you're joking."

"It's true."

"You're not going to tell me you've been a monk since your divorce."

"Not quite, but close."

His admission thrilled her more than it should. "You don't seem to have lost your touch."

"Maybe it's that old Costa Rican magic you were talking about."

"Could be," she said, swallowing hard. "It's pretty potent stuff."

"I'll say. 'Cause right now, despite my noble actions, I want you more than ever."

Dawn quickly dropped her gaze.

"Does it bother you to hear me say that?"

"No."

"Then what's wrong?"

"What's wrong is that I feel the same way."

Michael didn't say anything right away. Maybe he was testing the strength of her words just as she had done. "Let's go back to the hotel."

"Why?" she asked, a little too hastily.

"We both have rooms there, remember?"

"That's right." She laughed nervously. "I forgot."

Strolling back to the hotel, Dawn didn't balk when Michael slipped an arm around her waist. She didn't resist when he paused now and again to kiss her on the temple. Dawn would have been disappointed if he'd done anything less.

"Would you care for a nightcap?" Michael asked when they reached the lobby.

"We can't. The bar's closed."

He checked his watch. "Already?"

"It's off-season."

"Oh." He looked up and grinned beguilingly. "In that case, I have a couple of airline-sized bottles of wine in my room."

Dawn found herself mesmerized. Water from the nearby pool sent shimmering reflections onto the white-washed walls and across the blue-gray of Michael's eyes. "That's probably not such a good idea."

"Why? You don't think I'd do anything to hurt you."

She shook her head, having already considered and dismissed that notion. Michael looked wonderful, not at all threatening—except in the most enticing, masculine sense of the word.

"Nothing has to happen," he began.

"Unless we want it to," she said.

Michael smiled. "Exactly."

Cliché or not, she believed him. Nothing had to happen. Then again, maybe something would. Dawn was trying to come to terms with either possibility.

"Why don't you bring the wine to my room instead?" she suggested, as though it were a compromise.

"Okay."

"How about in half an hour? After dragging Enrique home, I could really use a shower."

"So could I."

"My room number is 238," Dawn said quietly.

Michael touched her cheek. "Perfect. That's one floor below mine."

As the two of them climbed the spiral stairs, Dawn noticed the night clerk standing nearby. She had no idea whether he'd been eavesdropping or whether he even understood English. But he was watching them now, and she didn't care much for the look on his face. Instinctively Dawn moved closer to Michael, a gesture that was feeling more natural every time.

FOR THE SECOND TIME that day Michael cursed the plumbing. When he'd showered shortly after check-in, the hot water was nonexistent, but the manager had assured him the problem was temporary. It was now eight hours later. Temporary was obviously a relative term, depending on the hemisphere.

Maybe it was just as well that he'd be visiting Dawn in a semifrigid state. He'd meant what he said, of course, that nothing had to happen. But that didn't mean desire wasn't there.

And desire was there all right, in spades. Michael couldn't remember when he'd been this captivated by a woman. His captivation, however, wasn't something Michael could easily explain. Dawn was lovely, yes, but not overwhelming. Her figure was exquisite, but understated—small breasts, slim hips—the kind of body that would age with grace.

Dawn Avery's finest attributes, he suspected, lay beneath the surface. Although they'd only been together a few hours, he had a pretty good idea of what they might be. Compassion, understanding, loyalty. He'd seen how she interacted with her friends, giving of herself without hesitation. Well, maybe she did hesitate once or twice with Enrique, but at least it was an honest reaction. And honesty was a rare trait these days.

Michael toweled off and dressed quickly. He was surprised, while buttoning his shirt, at the self-restraint he'd shown on the beach. He and Dawn could have been making love this very minute. He knew she'd been willing enough at the time.

But Michael was, above all, a gentleman. There would be no coercion, no underhanded tactics in his efforts to seduce Dawn Avery. He intended to rely solely on charm, sincerity—and whatever part of his physique appealed to her most.

After dressing he rummaged through the bottom of his suitcase. The occasion to use condoms had dwindled over the past few years, probably a sign of impending middle age. But he still kept them around. They were, he supposed, like an umbrella. Carry one around, and sure as heck, it'd never rain.

Michael took out four condoms and dropped them into his pocket. Then, for good measure, he added two more. Drought or not, it never hurt to be prepared.

NOTHING WAS GOING to happen, Dawn assured herself as she stood beneath the shower. It wasn't just a matter of trusting Michael. Trusting herself was just as important. And that, for Dawn, hadn't come easily.

After her divorce there had been frantic years when Dawn was terrified of being alone and unloved. She would wake up, sweat-drenched, in the middle of a nightmare. The details varied, but the theme was always the same. Dawn would see herself swatting mosquitoes and writing reports by kerosene lamp in some remote jungle outpost. It was virtually the same life she had now, but in the dream she was ninety years old— withered and bitter.

To counteract this terror in the daytime, Dawn would scrutinize and catalog every man she met as a potential partner. Not all of them became her lovers, of course, but the very process was exhausting and nearly destroyed her self-esteem. Life became a roller coaster of giddy highs and crashing lows, depending on whether or not there was a man in her life.

As time passed, the lows began to outnumber the highs. Except in the physical sense, men were no longer filling the void. Dawn didn't know where to find happiness anymore—or even whether it existed.

Finally, one morning, the precarious reality she had created collapsed around her. Dawn had awoken with a mammoth hangover—furry mouth, splitting headache, the works. She looked across her bed and nearly passed out. There was her new boss, the director of Montecristo's conservation league, snoring and naked. Not only did she hardly know him, she didn't even like him. What Dawn had once considered an independent life-style revealed itself for what it was—a giant case of self-loathing.

In that instant Dawn suddenly understood that she could never find happiness with a man until she was happy with herself. She had no idea how to begin the process, but gradually, as the weeks passed, answers came to her. She learned to release her fears and insecurities. With each release came a greater sense of confidence and a greater sense of love.

That was five years ago—in some ways, a lifetime. Dawn no longer fretted about the occasional absence of friends or lovers. The absences were never permanent. But in the meantime she always had her dreams, aspirations and the freedom of choice. Dawn had never been so consistently happy.

She stood in the shower, contentedly allowing the cold water to cascade across her back, shoulders, breasts. She welcomed the briskness, the tingling invigoration of her senses.

Dawn took a bar of soap and worked up a lather. Gliding her hands along her hips, she took pleasure in the subtle curves and smooth skin. Working in Montecristo often entailed miles of hiking, but the dividends of a firm body were worth it.

Moving upward, she cupped her breasts. Her nipples were hard, just as they had been when Michael touched them. With the memory so fresh in her mind, Dawn wasn't surprised at the arousal. She was, however, surprised by the added pleasure of reminiscence.

Thinking of Michael intensified the heat flowing through her. She turned to face the water and dropped her head back, smiling at the sensuous contrast of hot and cold. Lightly her fingertips retraced the course of Michael's kisses. Lips, tongue, and then the subtler places—earlobes, the sides of her neck, the hollow at the base of her throat.

His tongue, she recalled, had glided along her collarbone. His hand had rasped along the silken blouse, pausing at her waist, pressing gently. She'd felt his hunger mount and reveled in the feeling, as acute as hers. Both of them wanting, both of them holding back. Such a beautiful, exciting denial.

Humming to herself, Dawn picked up the soap again. She arched back and reached down to touch herself. She gasped. The cold water must have numbed her awareness, but there was no mistaking her physical state. The feminine parts of her were swollen and aching, just as they had been at the beach with Michael.

She moved her hand in small circles in rhythmic counterpoint to the rocking of her hips. With her other hand Dawn strummed fingers across her nipples, teasing them to full erection. Deep inside the pressure grew; the heat intensified. Dawn's breath grew shallow, and she squeezed her eyes shut.

She didn't need a man to enjoy her body. She'd long since mastered the delicious art of fantasy. But tonight, with the image of Michael dancing through her mind, the magic was heightened. It was *his* hand stroking, *his* touch that probed and thrilled.

Dawn dropped to her knees in the shower. Water streaming over parted thighs, she increased the tempo of movement across her tender flesh. Wave after wave of passion flooded through her body as Dawn conjured

Michael's mouth on hers. She could almost feel their joining on every level. He was thrusting deeper and deeper. Wanting her, filling her, calling her name in ecstasy...

"Oh, Michael!" Dawn cried out. Then, leaning back on her hands, she rode the last wave to repletion.

ROUNDING THE CURVE of the staircase, Michael nearly collided with the night clerk. The short, swarthy man was smoking a cigarette and leaning against the banister as though he'd been expecting him.

"Hello," Michael said politely.

The man grunted.

Oh, well, thought Michael, *we can't all be in a good mood.* He descended the last few steps to Dawn's floor. The clerk followed immediately behind.

Michael turned to him. "Is there something I can do for you?"

"No se puede visitar a la señorita."

"Sorry, but I don't speak Spanish." He was about to knock on Dawn's door when a hand clamped his arm. "What the hell..." He jerked his arm away.

"Es prohibido entrar."

Michael took a wild guess at the meaning. "I'm not allowed to enter?"

"No, señor."

"Says who?"

The clerk, scowling, gestured for Michael to return upstairs.

"Nobody sends me to my room anymore unless I—"

Just then the door swung open, and there was Dawn, looking sexy and radiant in a pale blue robe. "Michael!" She glanced at the dark-haired man beside him. "I thought I heard voices. Is something wrong?"

"I'm not sure. Did you hire a bodyguard while I was upstairs?"

"Of course not. This is the night clerk."

"I realize that. Why is he telling me I can't see you?"

Dawn shut her eyes briefly as though the situation wasn't entirely surprising to her. Why that should make Michael's stomach knot was something he preferred not to consider.

She turned to the Costa Rican and launched into rapid-fire Spanish. Michael couldn't understand a word, but he was grudgingly impressed with Dawn's ability to communicate. Her gestures, her cadence changed entirely. She became, while talking to the clerk, a Costa Rican.

As the discussion heated, Michael grew antsy. He could sense that Dawn wasn't making headway, and frustration at his own linguistic limitations wasn't helping any. "What's going on?"

"He won't let you in."

"I gathered that, but why not?"

Dawn didn't answer. She just switched languages again. This time the clerk shoved his way into the room and pointed to a notice on the wall.

Finally she shook her head. "It's no use, Michael. The hotel prohibits visits among the opposite sex."

"You've got to be joking."

"It says so right here. If you come into my room, management can call the cops and have you removed."

He uttered a none-too-pleasant oath. "But we weren't going to do anything." Then he remembered the condoms that now felt like bombs ticking away in his pocket.

"I tried to tell him we were just planning to, well . . . talk, but he said rules are rules."

Her tawny blush was appealing, but not enough to curb Michael's temper. "Where the hell do they get off making rules like that?"

"I'm sorry. I should have realized this might happen."

"You mean, this has happened to you before?"

"Not here, but in other Latin hotels, yes."

His jaw clenched. The knot in his stomach tightened. He couldn't trust himself to say anything.

"Why are you looking at me that way, Michael?"

"Never mind." So this wasn't the first time Dawn had issued an invitation to her hotel room. But who was he kidding? She had to be over thirty. And experienced or not, Dawn still appealed to him. A lot. "Can't we pay him off?" Michael suggested, half appalled to hear himself making the suggestion.

"Michael!"

He shrugged. "It was just a thought."

"Look, I'm really sorry."

"Yeah, me, too." Shoving both fists into his pockets, he turned.

"Where are you going?"

"Considering my options, where do you think?"

"There's no need to get angry at me."

"I'm not."

"You are."

Michael whirled around to face her. "Damn it, woman, I think my libido has undergone enough bashing for one night. I'm going to bed . . . to sleep, since it seems to be the only permissible activity around here. Good night, Dawn." He resumed his climb, bracing himself for Dawn's reaction.

Slam.

There it was. He didn't blame her one bit.

THE NIGHT CLERK LINGERED in the corridor. Within minutes he heard the sounds of two showers. One coming from room 238, a second from the floor above. The hot water was still off, so he knew they'd be cooling their passion pretty quick. Smiling with prurient satisfaction, he lit another cigarette and descended the stairs.

THE TIOGA'S OPEN-AIR RESTAURANT was one of Dawn's favorite places to eat. The large second-floor balcony overlooked swaying coconut palms and a white sand beach. The sky was already a brilliant azure—another perfect sunrise in Costa Rica.

But nature's perfection did nothing to appease Dawn this morning. Neither did the scrambled eggs and toast that were growing cold in front of her. She finished her coffee and checked her watch.

The first bus for Montecristo would be leaving in an hour. Not a long wait by normal standards, but for someone who'd lain awake all night, another hour was eternity. At least now it was light enough to go to the bus stop, and she'd be wise to leave right away. The other hotel guests—one in particular—would be coming down soon for breakfast, and Dawn didn't want to be around then.

It was inconceivable to her how one man, in one evening, could completely undermine her standards, challenge her morals and throw off her metabolism. She was thirty-five, for heaven's sake. Too old to be picked up in bars, too smart to invite a man into her hotel room and too levelheaded to regret that nothing had happened. But that was what Michael Garrett of the pinstripes and brogues had managed to do. And now she was actually sitting here missing him.

Dawn signed the tab, took her travel bag from beside the table and headed for the exit. Her heart was in her throat as she descended the stairs to the lobby. *Please, God, let me get out of here quickly before I see him again and do something else regrettable.*

But God must have had other plans. Dawn arrived at the reception desk to find a retired American couple signing out, the nit-picky kind who couldn't pay a bill without checking and rechecking.

"What's this, Martha?" The white-haired man jabbed a horny nail at the invoice.

"Just a minute, let me find my glasses." Martha had a straw purse from St. Croix that was larger than Dawn's suitcase. She rummaged through it for ages and finally dumped it out onto the reception desk. "What I need is a pair of glasses to find my glasses," she said, a joke her husband had probably endured a million times.

Meanwhile, he resumed arguing in pseudo-Spanish with the receptionist. "We did not order any of this im-pues-to stuff, sen-yor."

The man at the desk waved his hands in frustration. "That ees tax, *señor.* Tax."

The man blinked and turned to his wife. "What in the hell are tucks, Martha?"

Dawn couldn't stand it any longer. With a gritty smile she stepped up to her current source of aggravation. "That's room tax, sir. All hotels charge room tax—even in the States, I believe."

The man's face lit up. "Oh, you speak English! Look, Martha, she speaks English!"

Martha glanced up. "Wonderful! I think I left my glasses in the room."

Her husband didn't react. He was too busy jabbing at the invoice. "So what's this word mean?"

"*Desayuno*," Dawn explained. "That's breakfast."

"But I thought breakfast was supposed to be included."

"Only if you order from the standard menu. Prunes and oatmeal cost extra."

"They should have told us that first. Don't you think they should've told us, Martha?"

"Yes." Martha nodded knowingly. "That's the trouble with these foreign countries. You've got to be so careful they don't cheat you."

Dawn tightened her grip on the suitcase. "Where do the two of you come from?"

"New York City," Martha announced proudly.

Better cheated than mugged, Dawn thought with a groan.

It took another fifteen minutes before the New Yorkers were finally resigned to paying their bill, which contained not a single error. While they toddled off to their waiting taxi, Dawn moved up to the counter for her turn.

"*Hola, señorita.* Did you have a pleasant stay?"

"Very pleasant, thank you." Judging from the placid look on his face, he hadn't been informed of last night's fracas outside her room. Thank goodness, she could leave with some of her dignity intact.

She signed the bill, paid and was on her way out the door when the clerk called out. "I almost forgot, *señorita.* You have a message."

Dawn froze in her tracks, closed her eyes and toyed with the idea of ignoring him. The message had to be from Michael. It was probably an apology or a request for a date, something awkward and unanswerable. She'd rather forget she'd ever met him.

Well, that wasn't quite true. But this morning was too soon to run into Michael Garrett again.

The receptionist was not to be dissuaded. He ran outdoors and handed her the message. "*Gracias*," she mumbled—in truth, not the least bit grateful.

Then she read the message and laughed with relief. It was from Lito. Marisa had gone to the hospital in labor shortly after midnight. Everything was fine, so far. He would keep her informed.

"Good news?"

Dawn shrieked and dropped the note. "Michael!"

"Who were you expecting—Dracula?"

To her horror, she giggled—actually giggled—at his dumb joke. But he looked marvelous, freshly shaved and cool in a cream-striped shirt and tan slacks. "No," she said, "it's daylight, and I happen to know vampires hate daylight."

He seemed to be struggling over what to say next. "I missed you at breakfast."

"I ate early."

"I phoned your room."

"I wasn't there."

"Were you trying to avoid me, Dawn?"

Some questions, she realized, were impossible to answer graciously—especially when one felt obliged to be truthful. "No, I—that is . . . well, maybe . . ."

To her amazement, Michael laughed. She'd forgotten what a pleasant sound it was. Then again, maybe she'd never really heard him laugh. Everything had happened so quickly last night. How was a woman supposed to retain it all?

"I'm heading for Guanacaste," he said. "I checked the map, and it looks like Montecristo's on my way."

"Not exactly. It's an hour's drive off the highway."

"I can spare the time."

"The road's pretty rough."

"I can handle it."

His determined comebacks made her smile. Actually everything about him made her smile. Even in the sober light of day Michael Garrett managed to unnerve, charm, fascinate.

"So," Dawn said, "are you offering me a ride?"

"That's basically what I had in mind."

She held his gaze for a long while. If Michael's eyes had strayed one inch, if he'd given her even the slightest once-over, she'd have turned him down flat. But Michael didn't flinch. He faced her like a man of honor.

"A ride would be nice," she acceded with relief. "Thank you."

"Great, my car's this way." He gestured for her to go ahead. Then, dropping his gaze, Michael grinned. No doubt about it. Dawn Avery had an absolutely gorgeous set of buns.

4

THE INTER-AMERICAN HIGHWAY wove through central Costa Rica, an ever-changing panoply of mountains and ranchland, forests and valleys. Dawn knew the route intimately, yet never ceased to be enthralled with its beauty. Along with the enthrallment, however, came a recurring sense of frustration—of potential, unrealized resources squandered. So much needed to be done for this country, and so few people cared. It was probably no coincidence that Dawn's most inspired correspondence took place on this route while jouncing on the local bus.

But this morning conservation issues took second place in Dawn's mind. Competing with her usual zeal were new emotions, every bit as stimulating, yet harder to define. She only knew that Michael Garrett was the inspiration behind them.

Curiosity certainly played a part. Under different circumstances Dawn might have enjoyed getting to know Michael. But he was only going to be here for a week. It seemed almost foolish to expend the energy.

As for desire, it was there, too. Dawn had only to glance at Michael to recall the taste of last night's kisses, the warmth of his embrace. And she had to admit that, even in the light of day, he was a very attractive man. Dawn had half hoped that daylight would restore her to her senses, that she could regard Michael with some indifference. She wasn't faring well so far.

They were climbing out of a valley when Michael interrupted her thoughts. "Look over there," he said, pointing at a cloud of smoke billowing across the sky. "Do you suppose it's a forest fire?"

"No, they're slashing and burning."

"What for?"

"New pastures," she muttered, folding her arms.

"Let me guess," Michael said. "For beef cattle, right?"

"You got it."

"You really have it in for ranchers, don't you?"

"I have nothing against ranchers or farmers or grain producers, Michael. But I am in the business of protecting rain forests, and if these forests keep disappearing at their present rate, this planet isn't going to survive."

They drove for a while in silence. Then, just when Dawn was about to expand on her soliloquy, Michael spoke again. "Let me ask you something, Dawn. Are you concerned about the planet—or the people living on it?"

"That's an absurd question. Of course I care about the people living on it."

"If someone were to present you with a different approach to conservation, would you listen?"

She glanced at him cautiously. "Yes, I would."

"Good, because what I do is similar to conservation, but in terms of human resources."

Dawn's interest was piqued. "What exactly is your job?"

"Have you ever heard of loss control?"

"I don't think so."

"It's a relatively new field—and a vital one these days. In corporate jargon loss control means the maximization of profit through the minimization of loss."

"What does that mean in layman's English?"

"I'll give you a statistic that might help you understand. Every twelve seconds, in North America, someone becomes totally disabled in an industrial accident.
Every twelve seconds. In Third World countries the
numbers are even more appalling."

She drew in a deep breath. "My God, that's awful."

"It is. And, of course, those accidents cost companies
millions of dollars in compensation and lost time. Losses
which have to be recouped from other areas."

Dawn thought for a moment. "Which could include
the greater depletion of natural resources."

"Precisely."

Michael's argument, so far, was fascinating, if not entirely persuasive. "Where do you come in?" she asked.

"My job is to prevent those accidents from happening
in the first place."

"How?"

"By teaching people to care."

"It sounds like a catchy slogan."

"It's not a slogan. Accidents occur because of low morale, poor communication and unnecessary conflict between management and labor. We're talking human
behavior here, not mechanical breakdown. So it stands
to reason that if you turn their behavior into something
positive, you'll create an accident-free environment."

"But as you said yourself, Michael, you're dealing with
human nature. No offense, but one well-meaning con-
sultant can hardly change people's long-standing atti-
tudes toward each other."

"I have a briefcase full of evidence that says otherwise, and I'm about to prove it to Agrofin."

Dawn gasped. "Agrofin is your client?"

"Yes. Are you familiar with them?"

"Everyone around here is. Agrofin is owned by one of Costa Rica's wealthiest families."

"That's right."

"They also have one of the worst records for land expropriation."

"All the more reason for me to be here. If I can implement loss control and raise their profits accordingly, Agrofin won't have to rely so heavily on expropriation."

Dawn wanted to believe him. She wanted to believe there were actually people in the corporate world who cared. But she'd been disillusioned and disappointed too often to take him at face value. "What about layoffs? Will people lose their jobs because of what you do?"

"Sometimes layoffs are necessary."

His words were softly spoken, but he might as well have screamed in her ear. "Oh, I see," Dawn said, feeling suddenly vindicated. "It's called trimming fat, right? Improving the statistics. Never mind that these statistics have families to feed."

"Wait a minute." Michael's patience was also waning considerably. "I'll admit there are some downsides to loss control, as with anything, but what about your noble cause?"

"Montecristo? What about it?"

"Aren't you in the business of reclaiming land for the rain forest?"

"Yes, but—"

"The people whose land you reclaim, what happens to them?"

"They're given money to relocate," Dawn said with a touch of smugness.

"Do you keep tabs on the success rate of their relocation?"

"Well, not officially, but that's not our job. I mean, we're not responsible for . . ." Dawn didn't bother to continue. The look on Michael's face mirrored the hypocrisy of her reply.

Sliding lower into her seat, Dawn thought about the hundred hectares she had so triumphantly secured for Montecristo. Because of her success, peasant families who had worked the land for generations would be uprooted, their homes destroyed.

Maybe living in isolation had clouded her perception, but good intentions didn't change the inevitable. For every gain there was a loss. For every loss there was an incident of human suffering.

Dawn was realistic enough to understand she could never solve all the world's problems. She had no right to expect as much from Michael Garrett.

Entering the Montecristo region was like entering another dimension. Michael had found most of the scenery spectacular, but nothing like this final leg. The Tilaran Mountains, part of the Continental Divide, were steeper, more jagged than the coastal range. The rain forest was a tangled, towering mass with more shades of green than Michael had ever imagined.

And then there was the mist. It was sometimes thick, sometimes wispy, but so tangible one could almost touch it. Even when the windows were closed, he could feel the prickly dampness on his skin. The sensation wasn't unpleasant, but like mountain driving, it took some getting used to.

"We're almost there," Dawn said when they'd rounded another blind curve. "You're doing fine."

Michael didn't think he'd been that obvious until he noticed his white knuckles clenched around the wheel. "Guess you can tell I'm from the prairies."

"These roads are murder on everyone."

He sensed she might be saying that for his benefit. Dawn could probably maneuver these roads blindfolded. Still, he was grateful she'd allowed him his pride.

They were clinging to another hairpin when Dawn surprised him with an apology. "I'm sorry if I sounded kind of sanctimonious a while ago."

"No problem," Michael said, suppressing a triumphant grin. "You were just stating what you believed in."

"That's no reason to assume everyone else is wrong."

What a switch, he thought, from the woman's earlier bluster. "You're right," he said, "it isn't. But don't apologize for being dedicated. It's a rare enough quality these days."

"Thank you," Dawn said quietly.

When he'd had just about enough of the lousy gravel road, they reached the entrance of the Montecristo Reserve. A rotund security guard was manning the gates.

"That's Jorge," Dawn said. "He and his family are my neighbors."

Michael rolled down his window, and Dawn leaned across the seat to greet the guard. They chatted a few minutes, but Michael didn't bother trying to understand. He was content to breathe in the essence of Dawn's hair, mere inches from his face.

She didn't seem to wear cologne. If she did, it was pretty subtle. Clean, fresh, vibrant were the words that came to mind. But that, he was beginning to suspect, was a description of Dawn herself.

She finally said goodbye to Jorge, who waved them on with a friendly smile. When Michael pulled ahead, Dawn pointed to a small concrete building near the gate. "That's our administration office," she said. "Our houses are farther down."

The houses were more like cabins, small and wood-framed, clustered at the base of a sheer mountain wall. They were charming in a way, but amid the jungle surroundings they looked vulnerable, defenseless. Michael suddenly didn't like the idea of Dawn being here all alone.

"Who else did you say lives here?" he asked.

"The security guard and his family, the director and me."

"There's no one else on this entire mountain?"

"We're the only human residents, if that's what you mean. Our volunteers and part-time staff members live in the village."

Michael parked near a Land Rover with the Montecristo logo. "Wouldn't it be safer if you lived in the village, too?"

"I can't imagine why." Dawn reached into the back seat for her travel bag. "What could possibly happen to me here?"

"You could get sick," he said, tossing out the first thought that came to mind.

"We're all trained in first aid, and as you can see, we have a company vehicle to get us to the village."

"What about wild animals?"

Dawn laughed. "Montecristo has poisonous toads, but I've never known them to attack."

Michael was about to ask what they did in case of fire, but Dawn's curious expression stopped him. "Why this sudden interest in emergency situations?" she asked.

"I don't know. Guess I'm trying to understand how a person can survive in the middle of nowhere."

"I not only survive, Michael, I thrive on it."

He just had to look at her to know that was true.

"I thought you liked solitude, too," Dawn said.

Michael thought about his luxury condo near Winnipeg's Assiniboine Park. It was secluded in a way. Hundreds of people lived in the building, but he seldom saw anyone. "I do," he said, "but I prefer the urban variety."

"Wait until you see this place. You'll understand why I love it so much."

"I'm looking forward to it."

Dawn glanced at her watch. "My gosh, it's almost noon. How much time do you have?"

"Not much. I've still got some prep work for a dinner meeting tonight."

Her face fell. "So I won't be able to give you a tour."

"I'll be back," Michael said, surprised that his remark felt very much like a promise.

"Good. Do you have time for tea or coffee before you leave?"

Michael quickly weighed his options. "Sure, why not?"

He was curious to see Dawn's home. She was a scientist, so it would probably look like a laboratory, full of beakers and journals and pin-mounted bugs. Then again, given her social leanings, it might resemble something from the sixties with hanging beads and peace symbols. Hell, he didn't know . . .

Michael couldn't have been more off base. One word came to mind when he entered Dawn's cabin.

Erotic.

The first thing he saw—and practically fell onto—was her bed. This was no ordinary bed. It was a four-poster, ornately carved from some dark wood, and it occupied the center of the room. Draped from a brass ring on the ceiling was a canopy of gauze that extended to the floor— a mosquito net, no doubt. Cleopatra could have dallied here quite happily with her Nubian slaves.

"Do you like the bed?" Dawn asked. "I had it custom-made in Indonesia."

Michael cleared his throat. "Uh, it's, er . . . very nice. Good central location, too."

"I know it seems odd to have a bed in the middle of the room," she said, dropping her bag by the door, "but I'm cramped for space, so the bed kind of doubles as my living room."

Michael restrained himself from asking the next question. *If that's your living room, how much entertaining do you do?* Not that he wasn't itching with curiosity. He just wasn't ready for the answer he might get.

Dawn sidled around the bed. "Come on, I'll show you the rest of the place."

Michael had to tear his mind from sultry fantasies, including one of Dawn dressed in veils.

"This is my kitchen," she said, standing next to two straight-backed chairs and a sheet of plywood hinged to the wall. Her countertop and cupboards consisted of varying lengths of knotholed lumber.

The place might have looked like a shanty, if not for Dawn's decorating. The shelves contained brightly colored stoneware; above the table was a window with unusual lace curtains. Michael reached out to touch the off-white fabric. It was stiffer than he'd expected, both delicate and indestructible.

"What is this?" he asked.

"It's ñanduti lace from Paraguay, woven from plant fibers."

"Exquisite," he murmured, responding as much to Dawn's nearness as the lace.

She moved a few feet to the far wall. "Over here is my library."

Michael turned to look. The library was really nothing more than a wall of bookshelves with one overstuffed chair in the corner. But the books were an eclectic and revealing lot—everything from scientific journals to Anaïs Nin.

That Dawn was a fan of erotica shattered a few more of Michael's illusions. This was no cold-blooded scientist he was dealing with. What would she look like, he wondered, reading in her gauze-covered bed.

If the evening was warm, she might read in the nude, lying on her back with legs crossed, one slender foot swinging in the air. On a cool night she might snuggle beneath the covers, clothed in flannel with a cup of hot chocolate beside her. To his amazement, both images tantalized, and both images called for Dawn to put the book away. In his imagination Michael was beside her. Erotica might be wonderful, but a real man was even better....

Enough! Michael shook himself free of the fantasies that followed. If he didn't, he might never get away.

But Dawn still wasn't finished with him. "I'm especially proud of my wood carvings," she said.

Michael didn't know how he could have missed the collection on top of the bookshelf. The carvings featured men and women, some single and a few couples, engaged in passionate clenches. There were also statues whose sexual parts were effectively, and artistically, exaggerated.

"This is a pre-Colombian fertility god," Dawn explained, holding up one particularly virile male. "The more intricate ones are from India."

"I see." Michael felt himself turn hot and cold all at once. "You've really been around, haven't you?"

Dawn glanced at him, eyes twinkling with amusement.

Too late, he realized his double entendre. "What I mean is, you've traveled a lot."

"Yes, I have. Does my taste in art offend you?"

"Me? No! Well, maybe I was a little shocked, I mean . . ."

Dawn's amusement eased into laughter, but it was a gentle sound. "I'm not perverted, you know, and I don't collect these carvings to make people uncomfortable. I just happen to be fascinated with the human body."

Relief wove through his growing fascination. "That's understandable. You're a biologist."

She led him back to the kitchen area. "Yes, but there's more to it than that. You see, I've always believed that men and women were meant to enjoy their bodies—totally, without embarrassment—and that somewhere along the way we've forgotten how."

"I haven't forgotten," Michael insisted.

Dawn laughed again. "I was talking about humanity in general. We consider ourselves advanced, but some of our sexual practices and taboos go back to the Stone Age."

"So you think society should reexamine its attitude toward . . . uh, sex?" He was doing his best to match Dawn's nonchalance, but it wasn't easy. All this stimulation had him positively throbbing.

"Absolutely. It's wrong for us to associate sex with violence and sin. Even the animals know better."

"No doubt."

Michael turned to look at the carvings once again. Most of them, upon reflection, were truly beautiful. Far from being pornographic or shocking, they seemed to express a love more profound and natural than he had ever known.

"You've really given this topic a lot of thought, haven't you?" he said.

Dawn took a red-flowered teapot from the shelf. "Yes, I have, but there isn't much to do here in the evenings except think."

Her admission of loneliness caught him like a barb. A gentle hook that lodged irrevocably near Michael's heart. There was so much he could have said, so many ways he could have responded to Dawn. But he wasn't prepared for this onslaught of emotion, this sudden urge to protect and console. And so Michael resorted to something lame, noncommittal. "What's the weather like up here?"

DAWN COULDN'T BELIEVE the things she'd said to Michael. All that talk about mating practices and sexual taboos. No wonder five days had passed, and she still hadn't heard from him. The poor man must have thought she was an Amazon, or worse.

It wasn't as though she always behaved this way. Dawn had entertained guests in her home before, and once they got over the initial shock of her furniture arrangement, everything was fine. Her wood carvings were abstract enough that people generally didn't catch their significance. Why she suddenly felt compelled to shove them under Michael's nose was beyond her.

He had stayed long enough to finish his tea, but one foot was practically out the door the whole time. The more Dawn tried to put him at ease, the more uncomfortable he looked. When he finally made his escape, he didn't say a word about coming back to Montecristo. He just muttered something like, "See ya," which sounded to Dawn like the male paraphrase for "have a nice life."

On Friday afternoon she came into the administration office, feeling decidedly sorry for herself. Most of the staff had gone home for the weekend. Only the new director was still at his desk.

"Don't you know it's the weekend, Flavius? Time to let loose and enjoy life." *At least for some of us.*

He looked up slowly through steel-rimmed glasses. "I am enjoying my life."

"Oh, pardon me."

Dr. Flavius Van der Pol was a gaunt, bad-complexioned man who could have been anywhere between thirty and fifty years old. He was, as usual, writing in his journal, a dog-eared book that went everywhere with him. Dawn didn't feel comfortable enough with Flavius to ask what he was writing. He'd only been director of Montecristo for three months, and he wasn't a person who invited intimacy.

"Do you know if there are any messages for me?" she asked.

"None of which I am aware."

She knew better than to take him at his word. On scientific matters the Belgian was peerless. Regarding anything else, Flavius was beyond hope.

With a final trickle of optimism, Dawn checked the desks for any scrap of paper that might say, "Michael called. Will phone back."

Not surprisingly, there was nothing.

"This message you are expecting must be important."

"It is," she said, planting herself on the countertop. Flavius wasn't the greatest company in the world, but in

Montecristo one could hardly afford to be choosy. "Then again, maybe the message isn't important. I don't know anymore."

The director set aside his pen and folded his hands on the desk. "Could this be an affair of the heart?"

She nearly laughed at the archaic phrase, though coming from Flavius it was appropriate. "I only met the man once. I don't see how it could be."

"But he has obviously made a strong impact on you."

"I suppose so," she replied, swinging her legs unconsciously.

Flavius watched her legs, his eyes moving back and forth like myopic pendulums. "Perhaps he phoned and no one was in the office."

"That's possible, I guess."

In fact, it was more than possible. The only telephone in Montecristo was in the administration office, a decided disadvantage when it came to the pursuit of romance. But for Dawn romance hadn't been much of an issue lately.

"Where did you meet him?" Flavius asked.

"In a bar," she replied absently.

His nostrils flared. "A bar? Dawn, I am surprised at you."

Dawn waved a hand through the air. "It's not the way it sounds. Lito, a friend of mine, owns the bar. Michael was a customer there, and he and I just started talking."

"What is his background?"

"Background?"

"What does he do? Where is he from?"

Dawn looked at him strangely. She'd never known Flavius to take an interest in her life, or anyone's. But it probably wouldn't hurt to be open with the man.

"Michael is Canadian, a corporate type. Other than that I don't know much about him."

"He hardly sounds worthy of your affection."

Dawn laughed. "Worthy? What do you mean by that?"

"You are a scientist, Dawn, an expert in your field. It would be a shame if some . . . some man were to distract you from your life's task."

Dawn had spent a long, tedious day cataloging ferns in the forest. Yes, Michael had been on her mind, as he was every day. But he wasn't distracting. If anything, he increased Dawn's determination to concentrate on other things.

"I don't think my life's task is in much danger," she said. "Michael is supposed to be leaving Costa Rica today."

"Is that so?" Flavius licked his cracked lips. "In that case, would you care to have dinner with me tonight?"

5

IT HAD TO BE the most frustrating week of Michael's life. Not that the frustration was a total surprise. He'd known months ago, when Agrofin first approached him, that the job wouldn't be easy.

Family-owned companies required a deft approach, and the family that owned Agrofin and a dozen other subsidiaries was no exception. Agrofin's president, Carlomagno, was the spoiled youngest scion who'd been given the ailing feed and grain company as a test of his worth.

Carlomagno, to his credit, had recognized the severity of Agrofin's problems soon after taking command. He'd done well to contact Garrett Enterprises. False humility aside, Michael knew there was no one more qualified in the field of loss control than himself. To attract the best clients, he established his fee schedule accordingly. In the five short years that he'd been on his own, Michael's services had made him a wealthy man. But he *always* delivered.

That his reputation now extended to Latin America was a major business coup. No matter how daunting the task, Michael intended to save Agrofin from its own incompetency. After that, he surmised, it was just a matter of time before the rest of the Third World came knocking.

His first challenge with Agrofin had appeared in the form of Carlomagno himself. Michael had made a simple request, that organizational charts, achievement goals and cost projections be forwarded to his Winnipeg office. He had assumed they would be sent by courier or faxed. Instead, Carlomagno showed up in person with a valet who carried the documents and accompanied him on the family's corporate jet. Rather than conducting their meetings in Michael's modest office, Carlomagno reserved the Royal Suite at the Westin Hotel and ordered Dom Perignon and exotic hors d'oeuvres from room service.

In truth, the young Costa Rican's spending habits were of little concern to Michael. He knew the family's approximate net worth. They could afford to squander happily from now until the year 2000. It was Carlomagno's attitude toward Agrofin that mattered, and Michael realized early on that his attitude was rotten.

Virtually every loss control problem Michael had anticipated existed on site. His week at Agrofin revealed autocratic management, nonexistent training programs and low morale that filtered insidiously through the ranks. Little wonder that profits were slipping drastically.

Michael's frustration, however, wasn't brought about solely by Agrofin. He could have handled that. It was a woman, Dawn Avery, who had him climbing the walls at night, doing amorous things with his pillow and generally questioning his sanity.

She'd been on his mind incessantly ever since he'd left Montecristo. And no wonder. A man would have to be made of stone to remain unaffected by Dawn.

Michael had never bothered to take stock of his ideal woman. Tall, short, blond, brunette, the details didn't matter as long as the feelings were there. And over the years he'd experienced a lot of feelings. But ever since he'd met Dawn he had the uncanny sensation of something clicking into place, fitting perfectly.

Maybe he just had to get her out of his system, prove to himself she was only another woman, albeit an intriguing one. But something told him it wouldn't be that easy. That even if he never saw Dawn again, he would spend the rest of his life unconsciously seeking a woman with dark hair, green-gold eyes and legs that went on forever. Now there was a sobering thought, considering he wasn't even seeking.

Never mind the reasons or the risks. He had to see Dawn once more before he left. If the chemistry wasn't there, no harm done. He would write her off as a midlife fantasy. But if the chemistry *was* there—well, he'd cross that bridge when he came to it.

Michael tried all week to get in touch with her. Half the time there was no answer, but Dawn had warned him there was only one phone in Montecristo, and the office didn't have a full-time receptionist.

Twice he got through, but not to Dawn. He spoke to a man with a European accent. Michael had asked him to tell Dawn he wouldn't be able to get away during the week as planned. His schedule at Agrofin was too heavy. But if Dawn was available, and interested, he could change his flight plans and visit Montecristo on Friday evening.

All Michael needed was a yes or no. As he explained to the man, Dawn could either leave a reply for the next time Michael phoned, or she could call collect at his hotel in Guanacaste. The man promised to relay the message, but Michael heard nothing from Dawn.

Something must have gone wrong, he told himself Friday afternoon as he wrapped up his paperwork. Dawn wouldn't just *not reply.* She wasn't that kind of woman.

Then again, Michael had never met anyone who lived in a jungle on a mountain with erotica on her shelves. He couldn't possibly know how the creature thought.

DAWN STARED at the pimple-faced director. "I beg your pardon, Flavius?"

"I am inviting you to have dinner with me tonight. I prepare an excellent schnitzel."

"Why?"

"My mother taught me."

"I mean, why are you inviting me to dinner?"

His forehead bunched into little furrows. "We work together. Is it so unusual for us to socialize on occasion?"

Had he been anyone else, Dawn might have agreed that it wasn't unusual. But during the short time Flavius had been at Montecristo, not once had he made any overtures to the staff—friendly or otherwise. He spent much of his workday writing in his journal. He insisted on doing fieldwork alone, and in the evenings he would plod wordlessly to his cabin. Dawn noticed that his lights were often on until well past midnight, but she didn't have a clue what he did. Nor did she particularly care to know.

"I guess I'm just surprised at the invitation," she said.

"Then I will be honest with you. I have been observing you for months, Dawn. You are a fascinating woman. You remind me, in some ways, of my fiancée."

Dawn disregarded his awkward praise. "You were engaged?"

"Yes."

"What happened?"

"She deceived me."

"Oh, I'm sorry."

"Hmmph."

Sometimes, Dawn realized, the best way to bring one's problems down to size was to listen to someone else's. She had never imagined Flavius falling in love, let alone having his heart broken. She had to admit to a certain vicarious curiosity.

"Were you engaged for a long time?" she asked him.

"Four years. We were both students of biology in Brussels. We were planning to wed after graduation, but we never had the money. Then several years later Anna-Liise—that was her name—received a scholarship for advanced studies in England."

"It's difficult when you have to live apart," Dawn said.

"Geographic distance had nothing to do with our . . . parting ways."

"Oh?" she asked, trying to sound disinterested and concerned at the same time.

Flavius readjusted his glasses and lifted his journal into the air. "Anna-Liise and I were going to publish the results of this journal, a scientific study we had been working on for years."

"What kind of study?"

"The further application of Darwin's theories."

"You mean his theories of natural selection?"

"That is correct. We were on the verge of a major breakthrough. All we needed was the funding to test our theories in the field."

"You never got the funding?"

Flavius shook his head. "Not only that, Anna-Liise tried to publish our findings on her own—without my consent. But the study was incomplete and therefore inconclusive. We were ridiculed by everyone in the scientific community." He picked up his pencil and snapped it in two. "I have never, ever been able to forgive Anna-Liise for that."

Dawn had no doubts that Flavius was still harboring a grudge. His eyes were glassy, his face pinched. He looked as though he might implode. She also suspected it wouldn't be wise to linger.

"I'm really sorry about that," she said, "but I'm sure if you continue with your journal . . ."

Dawn was backing toward the door as she spoke, hoping that if Flavius looked up, he wouldn't be seeing the heartless Anna-Liise. To her relief, he didn't look up at all.

MICHAEL GRITTED his teeth and gripped the steering wheel, as though the combined effort might somehow keep him on the narrow mountain road. It must have rained during the week. The road was almost washed out in places, and the fog was like pea soup.

What had Dawn told him about mountain driving? The safest way was to follow the ruts, that was it.

Follow the ruts. Michael nearly laughed. Sounded like some people's philosophy on life.

The muddy tracks went straight down the middle of the one-lane road, which would make things tricky if he met someone coming the other way. But driving on the right didn't feel any safer. If the fog got any thicker or if he hit one good-sized boulder, he'd be over the cliff in no time. So Michael steered to the center and grudgingly stayed there.

This whole idea was stupid, he told himself, honking the horn while he rounded a curve. He had just spent five days doing battle with crooked executives and lazy foremen at Agrofin. Not only that, the mattress in his hotel was lumpy, the food intolerable and on Wednesday the radiator had seized up on his rental car.

He'd endured enough aggravation for one week without begging for more. And driving to Montecristo when he should have been on his way to the airport was definitely begging.

Michael was approaching another hairpin turn when he heard the horn. But it was too late. A tan-colored shape loomed through the mist. He locked the brakes and jerked the wheel to the right. Gravel sprayed. Mud splattered. Inches from the precipice, he stopped.

Dawn leaped from the Land Rover and rushed to the car at the side of the road. The mist was so thick that she could barely see the white vehicle. But she'd heard the tires skid, seen the backwash of mud and stones.

Heart in her throat, she peered into the driver's open window. "Are you all right?"

The man was gingerly rubbing the back of his neck. "I'm not sure... I think so."

"Michael, it's you!"

Wincing, he lifted his head. "Dawn?"

"What are you doing here? Your car... I didn't know... my God, Michael, you nearly went over the edge!"

Icy terror and relief battled for supremacy. Dawn began to tremble. She wrapped her arms around her midriff, but there was nothing she could do to temper the aftershock.

Michael quickly opened the door and stepped out. His head was pounding. His legs felt like rubber. He knew how close he'd come to cashing it in. But right now all he cared about was Dawn.

She was in his arms at once. "I'm so sorry, Michael. I was driving too fast, I should never have—"

"Shh, honey, don't." He held her close, stroking her hair with a tenderness that somehow assuaged his own fear. "It was my fault. I wasn't paying attention."

She looked up at him, eyes pooled with tears. "But, Michael, you nearly. . . I mean, you could have—"

"I didn't. I'm still in one piece, Dawn. See?"

He went through the pretense of squeezing a biceps. But his attempt at humor wasn't enough. Neither did his embrace confirm for Dawn what she needed to know. She reached up and cradled his face, nearly weeping at the warmth of his skin against hers. She traced the crags along his mouth, ran her fingers along his jaw, pressed his temple to feel the pulse.

Only when their mouths came together could Dawn truly accept that Michael was alive, unhurt. When his tongue dived deep into her mouth, hot and unbridled, she dared to believe he was here. His arms tightened around her waist, and she felt the sudden flare of his arousal.

It was bizarre, this mixture of passion and fear, but Dawn couldn't deny its invigorating pull. Her body moved against his hungrily. Her fingers roamed his chest, seeking and finding the rhythm of his heartbeat. It hammered with the insistent cadence of a man in need.

She needed him, too. She needed release from this tide of passion that rose and overwhelmed the deepest part of her. The trauma of the near accident paled beneath the fiery hue of Michael's kisses. The surrounding fog, prickly and cool, heightened the contrast of their heated bodies.

"Oh, Michael," she murmured, her lips against his, "I never thought I'd hear from you. I thought you'd left."

He showered her face with tiny kisses. "Oh, baby, I could never leave, not without . . ." Suddenly her words hit him, and he pulled back. "What did you say?"

His remark sliced through Dawn like a blade through silk. She stared at him, trying to identify the emotion in his voice. But all she could see was confusion.

"I . . . I never heard from you," she said. "I just assumed you didn't . . . care." Dawn had to force out the final word, in case he didn't. It was appalling to realize she could scarcely cope with Michael not caring.

"I phoned you half a dozen times," he replied. "I left messages."

"You did?" Dawn's heart raced, skipped a beat, then raced again. "No, you couldn't have. I checked for messages every day. There weren't any."

"The guy I talked to told me you were in the field, but he'd be sure to let you know I called."

Her blood froze. "Did he have an accent?"

"Yes."

"What kind?"

"I'm not sure. Dutch, maybe. But he had a deep voice and talked slowly."

"Flavius Van der Pol," Dawn said with deadly calm.

"What kind of name is that?"

"Belgian."

Michael clenched his jaw. "Who is he?"

"Our director. He only arrived a few months ago."

Maybe she should have suspected something like this. Then again, how could she? Until this afternoon she'd had no idea that Flavius was anything but eccentric. "I can't believe he lied to me."

"I'd sure like to hear his reasons," Michael muttered.

"I, uh . . . I'm not sure you'd understand them." Dawn saw no reason to enlighten Michael further. The question of Flavius's emotional stability was something she would deal with later.

"Thank God I found you in spite of that creep," Michael said.

Dawn was about to echo his sentiments when a new wave of panic flooded through her. "But when are you leaving? Wasn't it supposed to be tonight?"

"I changed my flight plans. I'm not leaving until Sunday evening."

"Is your...is your work finished?" she asked, not quite trusting her optimism.

"For now, yes."

"So you're staying longer just to . . ."

"Just to see you. That's right, Dawn."

She shook her head, incredulous. "I can't believe it."

"I said I'd be back, didn't I?"

"Yes, but . . ." She wasn't about to tell Michael she'd given up, not after he'd taken this kind of risk to see her. "But when I didn't return your messages, didn't you assume that I . . . well, didn't want to see you?"

Michael's eyes seemed to darken, revealing a determination and self-confidence Dawn could only envy. "I don't make those kinds of assumptions," he said. "And even if you didn't want to see me, I don't give up that easily."

The remark said a great deal about Michael's character. He had just as effectively stripped Dawn's pretenses. When she hadn't heard from him, she'd assumed the worst. She would never have garnered the nerve to call him at Agrofin or at his hotel. If Michael had behaved with the same cowardice, they wouldn't have seen each other again. They would never have . . .

But Dawn's thought had no ending. There was no ending because the two of them had yet to begin.

THEY WENT TO THE VILLAGE together in Dawn's Land Rover. First they visited the market to stock up on food for the weekend. Then they ate dinner in Dawn's favorite café.

The place was clean and simple with small wooden tables, whitewashed walls and a few copper ornaments modestly displayed. Dawn hadn't brought Michael there for the atmosphere. She brought him because the food was good and the prices reasonable. Only when they were seated and Michael glanced around did Dawn wonder whether she had done the right thing.

"This place reminds me of my favorite restaurant in San Antonio," he said.

"You've been to Texas?" she said.

"I conducted a three-day seminar there last year. It's a terrific city."

Dawn breathed a sigh of relief. She remembered now that he wasn't a snob. Things were going to be just fine.

Conversation flowed easily over steak sandwiches, french fries and beer. Michael shared with Dawn his failures and successes at Agrofin. The week had been challenging, and he'd made some inroads. But he had also fallen far short of his projections.

Dawn was impressed with his honesty. Michael could have cowed her with his corporate brilliance—real or imagined—and she wouldn't have known any better. She'd met enough men in her life who would do that.

But strangely enough, Dawn sensed that Michael needed to be honest. He needed to share his impressions of Agrofin and receive her unbiased opinion in reply. That she might prove useful to Michael filled Dawn with happiness.

"You shouldn't be so hard on yourself," she said. "It doesn't matter what kind of business you're in. Dealing with another culture is never easy."

Michael rotated his beer glass absently. "I don't know. The way things stand now I wouldn't be surprised if Agrofin ignored my suggestions and scrapped loss control completely. If that happens, my coming here was a total waste of time."

You met me, didn't you? Dawn glanced around as though someone had actually spoken aloud. But no one had. It was just a thought that had appeared, full-blown and audacious. She scrambled to get her mind back on track.

"But you said you're coming here again to do follow-up work, right?"

Michael, thankfully, gave no indication of having read her mind. "Yes, but if the Agrofin executives do refuse to consider my program, it's going to be harder to break through the next time."

Dawn could appreciate his concerns, and her empathy was genuine. But part of her was ecstatic. Michael Garrett was definitely coming back to Costa Rica.

THE OTHER SIGNIFICANT topic that arose over dinner was where to spend their two days together. Michael suggested driving to San José. They could book a suite at the luxurious Gran Hotel and tour the city in style.

For a minute or two Dawn entertained the notion. Heaven knows she hadn't been pampered that way in years. But it wasn't what she wanted. Not this time.

Dawn wanted to show Michael *her* world. She wanted to share with him every secret corner, every special treasure that Montecristo had to offer. There was the risk that he might not understand. He might find her passion for the rain forest ridiculous. But if that were the case, Dawn would rather know now—before his opinions really began to matter.

It was dark by the time they left the village. On the road to Montecristo they stopped to pick up the rental car where Michael had parked it on a secluded shoulder. Then he followed Dawn the rest of the way.

She used those few minutes alone to work out crucial logistics—the sleeping arrangements, for one. Her cabin was small, and she only had one bed. She could set up blankets on the floor, but this was the tropics, and the tropics were notorious for crawly creatures. Dawn wasn't afraid for her own sake. But given Michael's chivalrous nature, he would probably insist on taking the floor himself, and she'd be awake all night worried about him.

Sharing her bed was the only other option. The mattress was large, so if a man and woman wanted to maintain their distance, they could. But Dawn would be deluding herself if she thought it would happen. Not with the attraction simmering between them.

In truth, she wanted to be Michael's lover. She wanted to lie naked beside him, taste his kisses deep inside her mouth. She wanted him to touch her, hold her, cry out her name in sexual abandon.

Dawn didn't bother to speculate where this would lead because where it would lead was obvious. Nowhere. At the very most Michael might return to Costa Rica a few times during the next year. When his job with Agrofin was complete, she might never see him again. Time and distance, as always, would take their toll. And once again she would be alone.

But for the next two nights Michael would be with her. The next two nights were all she had.

The front gates were locked when they arrived, so Dawn used her key to let them in. She stood beside the gate and motioned for Michael to go through, then locked up behind him and drove the short distance to the compound.

The lights were still on in Flavius's cabin, reminding Dawn of a delicate and still unresolved problem. Damn it, he'd almost sabotaged this weekend for her. Somehow Dawn intended to ensure that it didn't happen again.

The security guard's house was dark. Jorge and his family had probably gone to the village for the weekend, as they often did. That meant the grounds would be quiet. Flavius seldom ventured out of doors after work.

Dawn parked the car and took a flashlight from her glove compartment. Heart racing, she stepped out, acutely aware of Michael only a short distance away. She watched him switch off the ignition and open the door. Then she saw his tall, well-formed silhouette, and her senses kicked into high gear.

Dawn became even more aware of everything around her. The temperature had dropped, the fog had lifted to reveal a beautiful starry display, and night creatures chirruped while her footsteps crunched as she crossed the short distance separating her from Michael.

The beam from the flashlight was directed at the ground, but Dawn's gaze was focused on Michael. He was watching her approach, and she felt her excitement intensify, as though his emotions and hers were blending. There was a brief moment of awkwardness, a suspended impasse when neither seemed to know what to say.

"I, uh . . . I'll bring the groceries in," Michael said.

"Okay."

"They're in your car."

"I know."

"I'll need the keys."

"Oh, right."

Nice going, Dawn. Keep wowing him with your brilliance. She held the flashlight while Michael carried the shopping bags. "Careful of the path," she said. "It's bumpy in spots."

"Thanks, but I'll be fine."

Dawn unlocked the door to her cabin and stepped inside first. Michael propped a bag on his thigh and groped along the wall. "Where's the light switch?" he asked.

"Light switch?" Dawn laughed, her tension suddenly relieved. "Even if I had one, it wouldn't do any good."

"Pardon?"

"I don't have electricity."

"Get out," Michael said, rooted at the door in disbelief.

"It's true," she said. "Didn't you notice the last time you were here?"

"Guess I was too busy noticing you."

Dawn turned to him in the darkness and smiled. "Wait there," she said, her nervousness giving way to warm anticipation. "I'll have a lamp lit in no time."

Michael could see Dawn in the soft glow of the flashlight, kneeling before a kerosene lamp. He watched her tip back the globe, strike a match and hold it carefully to the wick. Almost at once she was suffused in golden-white light. Just as quickly Michael was transfixed.

Dawn turned to face him, and the very motion made him ache. The lantern on the small bedside table had captured the highlights in her hair, creating a burnished nimbus of curls around her. The mosquito net over the bed provided a backdrop as fine as silken gauze. Dawn's lips were parted, glistening with moisture and the faintest hint of a smile.

Like a man possessed, Michael stumbled into the cabin. He dropped the groceries with an embarrassing clunk. Not since adolescence had he felt this helpless in a woman's presence. Then again, Michael had never wanted a woman as much as he wanted Dawn.

6

DAWN, IGNORING his impassioned state, stooped to pick up the grocery bags and carry them to the table. At first Michael felt abandoned. Then he realized that Dawn used kerosene lamps every day. She would hardly notice their ambience anymore.

Michael swallowed hard, shifting his jeans to relieve the worst of the pressure. He'd waited this long. He could wait another couple of hours.

"We have a generator at the office," Dawn explained as she stored the food in an insulated cooler, "but the cabins haven't been hooked up yet."

"When is that going to happen?"

"Whenever we have the money." Her tone of voice suggested that "whenever" could be a long time.

Michael noticed a small sink near the counter, but there were no faucets attached. "Don't you have running water, either?"

She looked up at him and smiled. "That depends on how fast you want to run for it."

"How do you live under these conditions?"

"It's not so bad once you get used to it."

A thousand emotions tumbled through his head. Michael was appalled that Dawn, a trained scientist, was forced to live in such primitive surroundings. At the same time he felt ashamed that he was so quick to condemn the place when Dawn's contentment seemed genuine. And most of all, he had this urge to shower her with every luxury and convenience money could buy. Not to impress her, but to make life easier. That last part was stupid. Yes, he could afford to indulge her, but Michael wasn't sure Dawn would even be interested.

"Don't you miss shopping and going to movies?" he asked, uncorking the red wine he'd bought in Guanacaste.

With the groceries put away, Dawn sat across from him. "I do my shopping in the village, and when I'm in San José I see the occasional movie. But I seldom crave civilization, if that's what you mean."

"What happens when you do?"

"I find some reason to go back to it...for a while." Her tolerant smile suggested that Dawn was no stranger to this conversation. "In all other respects I'm quite normal, you know."

Michael laughed. "I guess maybe I do have some misconceptions about reclusive women who live in a jungle."

"I understand. I used to watch *Tarzan* as a kid."

He sat and studied her a while, grateful that Dawn wasn't self-conscious. "You really don't mind it here, do you?"

"Are you kidding? I love it. But that doesn't mean I don't complain once in a while."

"Do you have any complaints now?" He reached out to play with a lock of her hair.

"With you here? None." She dipped her finger into the wine and licked it. Michael thought he would die.

"What about the way I kiss you?" he asked. "Does that meet with your approval?"

Dawn ran her tongue along her lower lip. "Mmm, mostly."

Michael took her hand and lightly sucked the finger she'd just licked. "What could I do to improve?"

The erotic gesture made her gasp. "You, uh...you don't need to improve, Michael. Just do it more often."

That was all he needed. Confirmation that Dawn's desire was as great as his own, her need to be loved just as—*hold it a minute.* Who said anything about love? Michael shook himself free of that last insinuating thought and concentrated instead on the present.

DAWN WAS BEGINNING to suspect she had lived alone too long. She had obviously lost all sense of judgment. Why else would she look into the eyes of a man she hardly knew and see love? Michael didn't love her. How could he?

He wanted her. Dawn had no problem with that. She wanted him just as much.

As a lover, she knew Michael would treat her gently. He would take his time pleasuring her, building the excitement until she cried out for him to take her. How she knew those things, Dawn couldn't say. Maybe that was what she had read in his eyes—and misinterpreted as love.

The most she could hope from Michael—all she wanted, really—was a night or two of ecstasy. And too much of this night had already passed.

"Would you make love to me, Michael?"

His mouth tightened as though he were restraining some powerful emotion. "Yes, Dawn, I would."

He took her hand. In a few steps they were beside the bed. Dawn drew back the netting and lapped it behind the headboard, then climbed onto the crocheted spread, inviting Michael to join her.

She reached over to dim the lantern, then closed the net, encasing them in a canopy of evanescent gauze. They lay together, face-to-face. Michael stroked her cheek, his gaze pouring over her, warm and wanting. "I was so worried I wouldn't see you again."

"So was I," she said, thrilled at the balance of their feelings for each other.

Dawn pressed her lips to the delicate skin inside Michael's wrist, and she breathed deeply. The scent of him was something she would never forget. At the very least she would always recall the effect it had. His essence was dizzying, intoxicating, utterly male.

"I'd have come here again, looking for you," he said, planting rosebud kisses along her temple and cheekbone.

"Would you? I'm so glad." Dawn shut her eyes and took a ragged breath. "I'd have written, but I . . . ooh, don't have your address."

His mouth was at the base of her throat, where Dawn could feel his words as well as hear them. "I'll leave you my address. Remind me . . ."

Then their mouths came together, and promises were no longer necessary. Dawn's hopes, fears and wildest imaginings were expressed in the movements of her lips and tongue. Michael was just as responsive. His lips understood her loneliness; his tongue expressed, without words, the feelings they shared.

As needs were emoted, needs were answered. Some of them, admittedly, seemed contradictory. Dawn had no delusions about her future with Michael. Yet, wrapped in his arms, she'd never felt safer. Part of her still struggled with her decision to become his lover; a greater part reveled in the choice she had made.

Michael slowly opened the buttons of her blouse. Dawn seldom bothered with a bra and wondered, with a quiver of self-consciousness, whether he would have liked the sensation of lace. But one look at Michael's eyes, one touch of his hands, and Dawn had her answer. He didn't need lace.

She arched back and cupped her hands around his head, leading him to her nipples. She needed Michael to soothe their ache, and just as much to intensify the feeling.

He didn't disappoint. With his teeth and his tongue, even the murmured vibrations of his voice, Michael lifted Dawn to new levels of delight.

She hungered to do the same for him. When her hands skimmed the fabric of his shirt, Dawn realized how sensitive he was. She had run her palms against his nipples, and now they were hard, pebbly, fully aroused.

Michael shrugged out of his shirt, and Dawn gasped at his strong, virile beauty. The broad chest, the thick mat of hair lightly tinged with gray. Impulsively she brought her tongue to his nipple and sucked.

His response was electric. He tangled his fingers in her hair, pressed her to him, moaned and whispered her name. Then Dawn climbed the length of him, and they kissed again, openmouthed, hungry. All thoughts of restraint were gloriously abandoned.

Somehow they disentangled long enough to remove the rest of their clothing. The sight of Michael, naked and erect, took Dawn's breath away. A long shudder rippled through her, a spontaneous, honest reaction impossible to suppress.

"You're exquisite," she whispered, realizing as she spoke that she had never uttered those words to a lover before. A deeper part of her knew that she never would again, except to Michael. But that was a premise Dawn chose to ignore for now.

He was in awe, his eyes almost worshipful as he took in the sight of her. His hands seemed to radiate an energy of their own. Stroking, caressing, Michael plied her with the attention of a caring lover.

When he reached across the bed for his jeans, Dawn panicked briefly, wondering what had gone wrong. But then he brought out the protection they would need. Dawn's fears were eased, at once, while her estimation of him grew.

She took him in her hands, astonished—and a little apprehensive—at the power of his arousal. Stroking him drove Michael wild. And with every stroke, Dawn felt her own body respond. Moistening, weakening, eager to surrender.

"I can't wait much longer," she murmured.

"It'll be soon, baby, I promise."

Lifting himself, he covered her body with his. Dawn felt the fit of his manhood between her legs and knew with staggering certainty that the fit would be perfect. But Michael wasn't ready to enter her. He still had more pleasure to give.

He climbed to his knees and ran his tongue down her body, pausing at her navel, dipping briefly. Then his mouth came to the moist, velvety core of her. With every frenzied movement of her body, Dawn thanked him. With every touch, every kiss, she was grateful that Michael had prolonged her ecstasy.

At some indefinable point, she reached a precipice and fell, a long, delicious tumble to sexual oblivion. Michael was there to catch her. He took her in his arms and entered her. Soon Dawn soared and fell again—this time not alone.

Michael was inside her, filling her with his passion. Dawn responded to every thrust, reveling in the feminine knowledge that she could satisfy. She clung to his back, appealing for more. Michael answered the appeal.

He gave of himself, and she accepted his giving. There were no half measures. Dawn cried out, overwhelmed. He filled her more deeply, and she cried out again. An eternity later Michael's shout of fulfillment joined hers.

They lay together, Dawn and Michael, two souls united. Gradually their repletion gave way to sleep. The mutual surrender was complete.

MICHAEL THOUGHT he'd awakened in a dream. He opened his eyes to a misty room, an ornate bed and a luscious woman. His body felt boneless, utterly content. He hadn't woken up feeling this way in years.

He reached out and touched the gauze as though to convince himself this was real. It was. So was the woman beside him.

Dawn was fast asleep, blissfully unaware of Michael watching her. She couldn't know how enchanting she was. With long lashes resting on her cheekbones, chestnut curls spilling across the pillow, Dawn looked totally at peace. She looked the way he felt, and Michael knew what had happened to make him feel this way.

Then a strange realization rippled through him. Dawn must look this way every morning, with the shadows of fatigue eased away, worry lines soothed by sleep. It seemed a shame that no one was waking to this sight every day. *And a damn shame it couldn't be you, Garrett.*

That was when a stronger jolt rippled through him. It could never be him who woke up beside her, no matter how appealing the notion. He only had one more night in Costa Rica. Then it was back to a snowy spring in Winnipeg.

Michael squeezed his pillow, struggling like hell to keep his hands to himself. He didn't want to disturb Dawn's serenity, not yet. He wanted to enjoy this moment as long as he could, capture it in his mind like a freeze-frame.

Dawn's lips were upturned slightly. She must have been having a wonderful dream. Was it about him, Michael wondered.

Then he shook his head, astonished at the effect she was having. This was supposed to have been a business trip. He'd long since given up the practice of bedding women when he traveled. But he'd broken his cardinal rule this time and with no regrets.

He should have been thinking about what to do with Agrofin. Instead, he was lying here thinking of Dawn. He should have been looking forward to going home. Instead, he was wondering how to wake her so that they could make love again.

"Good morning, beautiful."

At first Dawn didn't realize she'd heard the words. What she'd heard—or felt, rather—was the stroke of a finger along her cheek. Then the moist warmth of a kiss behind her ear. Every sound, every sensation wove through her dream like strands of silk.

The dream was unlike any she'd ever experienced before. She was running through snow, more snow than she'd seen in her life. The sun-sparkled whiteness extended forever, it seemed, across a flat, windswept expanse. Dawn didn't like cold weather, but in the dream she didn't even notice.

She was wearing a thick, furry parka and laughing delightedly at Michael's antics. He was making snowballs. No, more than that. He was fashioning them into huge blocks—building her a snow castle, he said. A castle for his queen.

She fell back into the white stuff and laughed again. *His queen?* What a silly, delightful, romantic man her Michael was....

"What's so funny, Dawn?"

Her eyes sprang open. Michael was propped up beside her, smiling. He was gorgeous. That was Dawn's first thought. Her second was that he'd catch his death of cold, lying in the snow naked.

But this wasn't a snowbank. This was her bed. They weren't in the Arctic, or wherever the dream had taken place. They were in Montecristo, the tropics.

Wakefulness and sleep swirled all around her, blending into a delightful concoction. Snowbank or rain forest, the venue didn't matter. Michael was her lover. And he was here, holding her.

"You look so happy," he said.

"I am." Dawn kissed his chin, then lifted her mouth higher for a gentle morning kiss. "That was beautiful lovemaking last night, Michael."

He nodded. "It was fantastic, honey." *The best I've ever known*, he almost said, but stopped himself in time.

Dawn didn't seem to notice the omission. She just burrowed more deeply into his chest. "I was having the strangest dream."

Michael lay on his back, stroking the swell of her breast. "What was it about?"

"You and I were frolicking in the snow."

He chuckled. "Frolicking?"

"That's the best word I can think of, which just goes to show how hokey dreams are. I can't stand the snow. You'd never find me rolling around in it."

"Winter's not bad once you get used to it."

Dawn shivered at the very thought of wind chills and drifts. "We lived in North Dakota when I was a kid. I was sick every year from December to March."

"I'm sure you'll adjust," he said absently.

She lifted her head and looked at him strangely. "Why would I have to adjust? It never snows in Costa Rica."

Too late, Michael caught his irrational slip of the tongue. "That's right, I forgot. So . . . are you as hungry as I am?"

LATER THAT MORNING Dawn was standing at the plank that passed for a counter, tipping a large plastic jug into a kettle. "Oh, darn, we're out of water."

Michael had just returned from the rest room at the administration office. He'd been able to shave and brush his teeth at a sink, but there were no shower facilities. Dawn had promised, with a lusty gleam in her eye, to show him the shower later on. With a promise like that, he was happy to wait.

"Do you want me to get some for you?" he asked.

Dawn grinned over her shoulder. "Sure. Do you know where?"

"The same place I shaved, right?"

"Yuck, you'd never want to drink that stuff. I get my water from the river."

Michael came over and took the empty jug. "Okay, then, how about you show me the river?"

It was more of a brook, really, that ran along the base of the mountain behind Dawn's cabin. The setting was unadulterated primitive. Crystal-clear water, a jagged slope tangled with lianas and tropical vegetation. The bird cries were primeval, haunting—unlike anything Michael had ever heard in Manitoba.

Dawn took the jug from Michael and stooped by the riverbank, her long hair spilling over her shoulders. He watched her humming to herself, performing the task as though she was born to it.

And as he watched, Michael found himself responding to Dawn differently. He suddenly felt protective, fiercely so. His eyes kept darting through the bush as though watching for unseen predators.

And he wanted her. Lord, how he wanted her. Right here, right now. His groin bulged and ached with a severity that made no sense, considering they'd made love half a dozen times since the night before.

Dawn stood up and turned, the jug of water in her arms. "Would you like to carry this?" she asked, smiling.

"Sure." Michael took the container and managed not to wince. The blasted thing weighed a ton.

"What would you like for breakfast?" Dawn asked when they were inside.

"You."

"Again?" She laughed. "You've got to be joking."

Michael was sitting at the table, chin propped on his hands, wearing an expression of total rapture. It delighted Dawn to realize she was responsible for that joy.

"I can't help myself," he said. "You are one incredible lover."

His praise made her knees weaken, and she groped for the table to steady herself. "So are you, Michael. How about pancakes?"

His smile faded almost imperceptibly. "Pancakes would be fine."

While Dawn mixed the batter, she had the feeling she'd upset Michael, disappointed him somehow. She couldn't imagine how. Their lovemaking had been spectacular. She'd done everything she could to give him pleasure, and Michael had done the same. What more was there?

Love.

Dawn cleared her throat, as though to dislodge the very word. Of course, love would be nice. Everybody wanted it in some form or another. But her life was hardly conducive to the time-honored traditions of dating and commitment. She was already committed to a goal that went beyond personal consideration. Surely he understood that and wasn't expecting more.

The simple truth was that she and Michael had just spent the first of two nights together. Half their time was already gone. There would be no opportunity to explore love, let alone discuss it. And as far as Dawn was concerned, that was just as well.

AFTER BREAKFAST they lingered over coffee with the glorious insouciance of new lovers. Dawn had decided she must have imagined Michael's earlier disappointment. He'd been nothing but charming, attentive and witty while they ate. Dawn had done her best to be the same.

"So when do I get my official tour of Montecristo?" he asked.

"Anytime you like," she said, running her fingertips along his forearm. He was wearing jeans and a dark blue polo shirt. The color suited him, enhancing the blue-gray of his eyes. But most of all, she loved the way the clothes hugged his body and left his arms bare. So many of Michael's physical attributes were missed in those regulation pinstripes. Thank goodness she'd finally gotten past them.

"Tell me if I'm wrong," Michael said, pressing her hand to his arm, "but you don't seem nearly as determined to show me this place as when we met."

Dawn chuckled. "You're right. I'm not. I think my passion has been temporarily diverted."

"Only temporarily?"

There it was again, that look. Michael's mouth was turned upward, but the smile was unconvincing. What Dawn saw instead was vulnerability, anticipation and some deeper emotion she preferred not to define. Didn't he know better than to reveal those things, especially to a woman like her?

Dawn turned her head away and grabbed a couple of bath towels from a nearby cupboard. "Let's go for that tour. And I promise you this one is tailor-made."

The forest always had a palliative effect on Dawn. No matter how irritated, lonely or frustrated, she could always come out here and find reprieve. This morning was no different.

Yes, it was, she corrected herself. This morning *was* different. Michael was with her, holding her hand as she followed the familiar winding pathways. And this time she was neither irritated, lonely nor frustrated when she walked beneath the towering green canopy. She was happy. And that happiness had somehow heightened every color, sound and texture that made up Montecristo.

Michael, she could see, was unprepared for the stunning beauty of the rain forest. Every orchid, every butterfly left him at a loss for words. That pleased Dawn. When she first saw this forest, her reaction had been exactly the same.

"It's like Eden," he said, kneeling to examine a pale green fern. "I can't imagine actually working here."

Dawn dropped to her knees beside him. "I can't imagine working anywhere else."

He looked up at her, his gaze moving from her eyes to her mouth, then back again. He wanted to kiss her, Dawn surmised. She wished he would act on the impulse.

"What exactly is your work?"

She had to think a moment, disentangle herself from the complex emotions Michael was evoking. "I do a thousand different things—most of them tedious, the rest of them frustrating." Then she laughed. "I don't mean to sound dissatisfied. It's just that being a field biologist implies a lot more than picking orchids."

Michael spotted a fallen log. "Let's sit over here, and you can tell me everything."

Dawn couldn't remember when she'd had a more captive, or impartial, audience. It felt wonderful to talk with Michael about her life. She described her endless hours of cataloging in the forest. Every species of flora and fauna had to be meticulously accounted for. Occasionally new species were discovered, and that was always cause for celebration. More tragically others—because of pollution and various factors—were declared extinct.

She told him about the tours she conducted for so-called "eco-tourists," travelers who were interested mainly in ecology and conservation. The tours could be frustrating, since they disturbed animal habitats and detracted from valuable research time, but they were also a blessing. Many of the tourists who visited Montecristo were inspired to "purchase" hectares of land and donate them to the reserve. They also took home with them a new understanding of rain forests and their crucial contribution to survival.

"There's always a backlog of reading and correspondence," Dawn went on to explain. "We have to keep up with new scientific developments—everything from zoology to forestry. And it's important to stay in touch with Montecristo's supporters so they don't lose interest."

Michael shook his head. "Sounds like a constant struggle for survival."

"That's exactly what it is," Dawn said sadly. "Like the forest itself. But the job I hate most is politicking, trying to persuade bureaucrats and politicians and businessmen to take an interest in this forest. We need protective legislation, we need cooperation from businesses and we need money. Most of all, money."

He took her hand and wedged it in a warm place between his thighs. "Montecristo is really important to you, isn't it?"

She looked up with eyes as green as the jungle. "Montecristo is my life, Michael."

He had no doubts about her sincerity. What he couldn't understand was his own reaction. For the third time that morning he felt as though Dawn had somehow turned him down, rejected him—when he knew damn well he hadn't made an offer.

THEY WALKED FOR HOURS, it seemed, along trails that dipped and climbed, meandered and sometimes disappeared altogether. They saw hummingbirds, macaws, umbrella birds and tiny golden toads that lived only in Montecristo. Dawn had hoped to show him a quetzal, the rarest bird of all. To see one was considered a sign of divine blessing, but so far it had proved elusive.

The beauty of the rain forest was dramatic, so all-encompassing that Michael could almost believe there was nothing worthwhile outside of these boundaries. How could a person look at traffic, pollution and crime the same way after he'd had a taste of Montecristo? He'd go stir-crazy living here. But he was beginning to understand Dawn's determination to save the place.

Meanwhile, Michael was feeling the effects of the fresh air and exercise. He waved his arms in mock surrender, then collapsed against the trunk of a giant fig. "Whoa, we've got to take a break."

"But we're almost there."

He lifted a cynical eyebrow. "Almost where?"

"At the shower."

"Get out," he said. "You don't hike all this way just to wash up."

Dawn laughed. "No, there's a shower house behind Jorge's. But once in a while I like to come out here and indulge myself." She reached up with a towel and wiped the sweat from his forehead. "And this morning I feel like indulging you."

Michael pulled her closer. Then he laced his fingers through Dawn's hair and kissed her. "Guess I'll have to trust you on this one."

They walked for a few more minutes, then Michael heard a roaring sound ahead of him. If he didn't know better, he'd have sworn it was a locomotive bearing down on them. But the volume and intensity didn't change, except as they got closer.

Dawn, meanwhile, was smiling, her eyes getting brighter every second. She looked like a little girl who'd planned a special surprise and couldn't wait to show him.

Then the forest opened up like curtains on a stage, and Michael found himself face-to-face with the most breathtaking spectacle he'd ever seen. It was a waterfall, maybe a hundred feet high, ten feet wide, cascading down a vertical rock wall. Lush jungle foliage flourished on either side—rubber trees, dracaenas, flowering vines. At the base was a pond, foaming near the falls, calm and crystal-clear in the center.

Lost for words, he turned to Dawn. She was smiling at him, looking serene and utterly radiant.

They would soon be making love beneath this waterfall. Michael knew that as well as he knew his own name. What he didn't understand was this almost overwhelming urge to fall to his knees and thank whatever powers had led him to this place . . . and this woman.

7

DAWN HAD SELDOM seen reverence on a man's face. She had certainly never inspired such an emotion. But that was what she perceived in Michael's gaze. He was watching her from the edge of the clearing, his hand resting on a branch, eyes shimmering with rapture, tenderness, adoration.

Incredibly, when she looked at Michael, she recognized those same feelings within herself. How two people could mirror each other's sentiments with hardly a word between them was something Dawn couldn't comprehend. But whatever the source of this bond, she trusted it.

Dawn draped her gunnysack over a tree, then approached Michael slowly. His eyes flickered, his smile was tremulous. But he didn't move, and that pleased Dawn. She wanted to be the initiator this time, the first to give pleasure. His tacit acceptance was a delight.

First, she cradled Michael's face in her hands and kissed him. Lightly, tenderly. His body was trembling with barely controlled passion, but she knew his strength. She knew Michael would allow her to release his passion in small measures, and thereby enhance their enjoyment.

She used her tongue to define his mouth, skimming the subtle bow of his upper lip, the rosy fullness of his lower. Then she sucked lightly on each, drawing the delicate flesh into her mouth and flicking her tongue against it.

At the same time she slipped her hands beneath his shirt and lifted them to his nipples. Already erect, they hardened even more on contact.

"Oh, Dawn, when you touch me there . . ."

"Does it feel good?" she whispered.

"Yes, yes . . . no woman has ever bothered . . ."

A flicker of anger rose inside Dawn—inspired not by jealousy but resentment that other women hadn't loved Michael as he should be loved. But she was also thrilled to learn she was the first.

Circling his areola with her fingertips, Dawn felt the immediate response at his groin. It was as though unseen strings bound the pleasure points of his body. All she had to do was strum them.

Instinctively Dawn realized she could bring Michael to climax with her hands and mouth, but this wasn't a display of sexual supremacy. She wouldn't deprive them of what lay ahead.

Removing Michael's shirt, she stepped back, giving him a minute to catch his breath, and herself a chance to admire. He was an exquisitely proportioned man, one who was just reaching the peak of his physical attraction. The angular contours of youth had filled out, broadening his chest, strengthening his torso. His chest hair was like a thick, sensuous mat just made for a woman's hungry hands.

"Let me undress you, Dawn."

"Not yet, darling . . . not yet." It was unlike Dawn to use endearments with a lover, but with Michael the words felt totally natural. As natural as the waterfall and the spirited chirrup of birds.

She moved closer again and knelt to unbuckle his belt. He groaned when her hand rubbed along the bulging denim, and Dawn's body responded in kind. She was throbbing inside, hot and damp from wanting him. It required all of her efforts not to tear the clothes from his body and let nature have her way.

Slowly Dawn lowered his jeans. Michael placed both hands on her shoulders and, with shaky legs, stepped out of the restrictive denim. His briefs couldn't contain his arousal, and Dawn breathed in sharply at the sight. Removing his briefs, she was careful not to touch him, knowing how close they both were to losing control.

She wanted this to be perfect, and to happen not a moment too soon. Dawn climbed quickly out of her clothes, her eyes dancing over Michael as they drank in each other's nudity.

"Lord, woman, you are the most beautiful . . ."

Dawn believed him, not because she considered herself a beauty, but because there were times when beauty shone through, regardless of a woman's self-perception. This was such a time.

"So are you, Michael . . . so are you."

She cast aside her lacy panties. Now they were both naked, as shameless and honest as the first two people on earth. Dawn nearly cried out with joy. *This* was what she had been striving for in her careful disrobing of Michael. She didn't want the social trappings of seduction, not this time.

There was no candlelight in these woods, no expensive wine or romantic music. There was only nature. And Dawn wanted nothing more than to be a woman for her man.

Something in Michael's expression told Dawn he understood. He was no longer trembling, no longer on the verge of losing control. He was very much aroused but fully confident when he reached for Dawn.

Hand in hand they ran toward the water. Together they entered, laughing and shrieking as their bodies adjusted, two playful creatures enjoying nature's gifts.

When they tired of their antics, they dived underwater and swam toward the base of the waterfall. Michael was a strong swimmer; so was Dawn. They kept up with each other easily. When they surfaced, they were at the base of the falls, exactly where Dawn had hoped they would be.

The water, glistening and tingly, sprayed their bodies. The churning whitecaps made them dizzy, and at first they laughed in sheer delight. But as they reveled in the glorious naked perfection of each other, laughter subsided. In its place rose another kind of joy.

Michael cupped Dawn's waist, steadying her. Then he stepped forward and pressed his body to hers. The embrace was slippery and wet, as were his kisses. But while his skin was cool from the towering cascade, Michael's kisses were steamy, evocative of the desire simmering within them.

"I've never felt anything like this, Dawn."

"Nor have I," she replied truthfully. She had come to the waterfall countless times, fantasized about being here with a lover. But fantasy could never compare with the sensations of Michael holding her, loving her.

His hands stroked up and down the glistening length of her, pausing at strategic places to arouse and excite until Dawn thought she would burst. Then he stooped to take a nipple in his mouth. With his hand he cupped the aching, submerged core of her.

"I want to be the best," he murmured, his voice barely audible above the roaring falls. "The best you've ever had."

Dawn arched back to give more fully of herself. "You already are, Michael . . . you are the best."

"Tell me what you want," he said. "Tell me how to love you." He had reached deep inside her, probing the very depths of her need. Dawn was so weak from wanting that she could scarcely stand.

"What you're doing is . . ." She gasped and threw her head back. "Oh, Michael, it's just beautiful! Love me however you like."

There was a large rock near the maelstrom of the falls, its smooth surface barely visible above the foam. Gently Michael turned Dawn around and led her to the boulder. Tenderly he lay her upper body across the surface.

It was remarkable, but the contours of the rock seemed specially designed to hold a woman. Dawn's breasts were cupped, her legs supported against grooves along the side. Water sprayed and danced across her back while Michael slowly lowered himself and entered her from behind.

She had never been loved so deeply. In this position, that somehow felt mystifying, primeval, Michael reached places that Dawn had never known existed. When he reached those places, slow and tender was not enough. She needed him to love her hard.

He did.

Dawn climaxed more strongly than she could remember. Clawing the rock, she could hear herself scream, responding to feelings that were wild, feral, totally beyond her range of experience. Once or twice she glanced over her shoulder to look at Michael. His head was thrown back, eyes squeezed shut while he thrust himself inside her with joyful raw abandon.

In this secluded paradise Michael was the aggressor, the epitome of outward masculine energy. Dawn was the receptor, purely feminine, all woman. They were male and female, positive and negative. As with the universe, their balance was perfect.

THEY SPENT ALL DAY at the falls. Dawn had packed a lunch of bread, cheese and fruit. There was plenty of fresh water, and the sun was warm. There was no need to hurry home.

Dawn was leaning against a broad-leaved tree. Michael lay with his head on her lap, feeding her lush red grapes. It was late afternoon, and they'd just finished making love again. Their bodies were sated, their minds at peace.

"I can understand how Omar Khayyám was inspired to write the *Rubáiyát*," Dawn remarked, chewing thoughtfully on a grape.

"Come again?"

"The *Rubáiyát*. It's a collection of ancient love poems. They're so romantic, you should read them..." Dawn stopped herself and laughed almost shyly. "Now you know how I get through those long, lonely evenings."

Michael's eyes seemed more blue than gray, as clear as the sky overhead. "Is it enough for you, Dawn, to read love poems?"

"Usually."

"What do you do when it's not enough?"

Her truthfulness astonished her. "Sometimes...I cry."

FLAVIUS VAN DER POL was scuttling across the grounds, journal under his arm, when Dawn and Michael emerged from the forest.

"Who's that?" Michael asked.

"Our director, the one you talked to on the phone."

Michael's face tensed. "I think I'd like to meet that man."

There wasn't time to warn him about Flavius. Even if there had been, Dawn wouldn't have known what to say. She was still reeling from her disturbing encounter the day before.

She practically had to step in his path to get the man's attention. "Hello, Flavius."

He looked up, his eyes bleary. "Good day."

Dawn turned to Michael. "This is our league director, Flavius Van der Pol. Flavius, this is Michael Garrett."

The two men shook hands, but it was hardly an amicable greeting. Michael looked as if he wanted to throttle Flavius, and the Belgian looked cornered, as he always did.

"I believe I've spoken to you on the phone several times," Michael said.

Flavius blinked slowly. "I don't recall."

"Sure you do. I asked you to pass a message to Dawn. I called from Guanacaste."

There was no sign of recognition. He merely clutched his journal more tightly. "You must be mistaken. I have no time for phone calls. I have been working on a major scientific project, as Dawn knows, and I must also prepare for a symposium in Brussels."

"What symposium?" Dawn asked, puzzled.

"The Future of the Planet. You must have heard about it. All the greatest minds will be present—Sagan, Hawking—and I am to be one of the speakers." He reached into his journal and pulled out a brochure. "See, here is my name on the back."

Dawn stared at the faded brochure. First she went numb, then a shudder ran through her. She glanced at Michael to catch his reaction. But he was obviously unaware of the problem and still steaming from Flavius's denial of the phone calls.

"I would invite you to come along, Dawn," her director continued, "but someone must look after Montecristo and I do trust you, as always."

"You t-trust me?" she stammered, linking her arm around Michael's. "That's nice to hear, Flavius. Good luck with your, um . . . speech. Let's go inside, Michael."

Michael looked as though he'd have preferred to continue this discussion, but she yanked his arm insistently. "I'm sure Flavius is right," she said. "There must have been some mix-up over the phone calls. You probably talked to Jorge."

Michael stayed quiet until they were in the house. Then he exploded. "That jerk is lying. I know who I spoke to on the phone."

"So do I. You spoke to Flavius."

"Then why the hell did you let him deny it?"

"Because..." Dawn sat down and expelled a long, deep breath. "You know that symposium he said he's preparing for?"

"The one in Brussels? What about it?"

"The symposium is long gone, Michael. It took place two years ago."

MICHAEL HAD BEEN PACING the cabin for nearly half an hour, no easy task considering the layout. Dawn watched him follow the walls—straight ahead, to the right, forward and left—while her own agitation increased.

"Can't you at least go counterclockwise for a while?" she snapped.

He stopped, midstride. "My pacing isn't the problem. Your living on a mountain with a nut case is."

"I know Flavius is unbalanced," she said, resuming an argument they'd begun earlier. "I just don't know what to do about it."

"You have to get rid of him. There's no choice."

"But he's my boss!"

"Even bosses are accountable."

Dawn drew her knees to her chin, knowing he was right and feeling utterly disconsolate.

"Who is his superior?" Michael asked gently.

"He reports to a board of directors in San José."

"Then all you have to do is contact the board and inform them of what's happening."

"It's not going to be that easy."

"Why not?"

Dawn felt the blood drain from her face. Her stomach was clenched in a painful, burning knot. She hadn't felt this way in five years. She had hoped—naively, perhaps—never to feel like this again. "Because the board might not believe me," she said in a small voice.

Instead of resuming his trek around the room, Michael came and joined Dawn at the table. "You're the most honest person I've ever met. Why wouldn't the board believe you about Flavius?"

Before she replied Dawn quickly calculated her options. She and Michael only had one more night. If she lied, they could probably spend their remaining time together with Michael none the wiser. If she told him the truth, he might be so repelled that he'd leave for San José at once. Both alternatives were risky, and both were going to hurt like hell.

Finally Dawn made her choice. If honesty was a virtue that Michael admired, the least she could do was keep hers intact. If he never saw her again, at least he would remember that, at the end, Dawn Avery had told him the truth.

"IT'S A LONG STORY," she said with a sigh. "Are you sure you want to hear it?"

"Under the circumstances, yes."

"You're not going to like it."

"Why don't you let me form my own opinion?"

Michael was right. He was entitled. So Dawn took another deep breath and began. "Five years ago, soon after I arrived in Montecristo, we got a new director."

"Isn't Flavius new, too?"

Her mouth twisted into a grim smile. "The director's job is a thankless one. It has a high turnover. Anyway, this fellow was Costa Rican, and he came from a very influential family."

"Was he qualified?"

"Not really. He had the right educational credentials, but he considered this post a stepping-stone to a political career. He used to brag about making Montecristo famous and then running for president."

"It doesn't sound like you liked him much."

"I didn't," she admitted. "At first I tried to get along with him. Everyone did. But he was impossible to like. He was rude, overbearing and totally unsuited for the life-style at Montecristo."

"What happened to him?"

Dawn stared at the wall, focusing hard on a knothole. "He resigned, but he should have been fired."

"Why wasn't he?" Michael asked.

"Because . . . because if I'd pushed it, I might have lost my job, too."

"Why, Dawn?"

"I slept with him."

MICHAEL FELT as though he'd been shot. He wouldn't have been surprised to look down at his chest and find a gaping hole where his heart used to be. But that didn't make sense.

So Dawn had slept with a guy, one she didn't like very much. That was five years ago. Big deal. It shouldn't have mattered. But, damn it, it did matter. And that was the part that felt like a bullet through his chest.

"I'm not sure I want to hear any more," Michael said.

"What? You practically dragged this story out of me! The least you can do is hear me out."

He stared at Dawn, his jaw clenched. He knew this was the same woman he'd made love to less than an hour ago. The caring, the gentleness, it was all there. But there was something different about her now, something banal and desperate and terrified. If Michael stayed and listened to the rest of Dawn's story, he wasn't sure he could like her anymore.

She didn't give him the option. "It goes back farther than Montecristo. After my divorce I went through some awful years. I resented my husband and wanted to take out my resentment on every man I met."

"By sleeping with them?"

Dawn flinched, but to her credit she looked him straight in the eye. "Sometimes . . . certainly more often than I should have."

Michael could have consoled her. He could have told Dawn that he'd done virtually the same thing after his divorce. But the wound she'd inflicted was stinging too much. And so he said nothing.

"When I, uh . . . when I finally got the job in Montecristo, I had no self-esteem. None. I not only hated my ex-husband, I hated myself and most of the world, I suppose. I hoped that by living here in the middle of nowhere things would improve."

Despite his efforts, Michael could feel his resistance being chipped away by her honesty. "Did things improve?"

"At first I thought so. I stopped going out, stopped drinking and I immersed myself in work."

Dawn had a fist pressed to her mouth. Michael suspected she didn't even notice the teeth marks she was making.

"What went wrong?" he asked.

"I got lonely. I didn't know how to live with myself. Every night I'd pace this room and want to smash everything in it." There were tears in Dawn's eyes, but Michael knew she was trying her damnedest to ignore them. "One night I couldn't stand it anymore. I knocked on the director's door and asked him if he wanted to go out for a drink. I thought if I just had someone to talk to—it didn't matter who—I'd be okay."

"Why'd you invite him?"

"There was no one else around."

"Go on," Michael said, his chest tightening.

"We went to a bar in the village. He bought a bottle of expensive Scotch. That was to impress me, I suppose, but I don't even like Scotch. We must have finished it . . . I don't remember." Dawn's gaze was boring a hole through the table. "The next thing I knew I woke up in bed with a splitting headache and that jerk of a director lying beside me."

Michael blew out a long breath. "You have no idea how he got there?"

Dawn shook her head. "The last thing I remember was laughing at something he said in the bar and realizing, as I laughed, that he thoroughly disgusted me. You can imagine how I felt in the morning."

Even now the memory of that day haunted her. It was, without a doubt, the low point of Dawn's life. She had crawled out of bed, staggered outside and immediately begun to vomit. For nearly an hour she lay on the ground, retching, until there was nothing left—not even hatred.

"Did you blame him for what happened?" Michael asked after allowing himself a minute to regain control.

"No, of course not. Whatever happened, I'm sure he didn't have to break into my cabin."

Dawn fell silent to collect her thoughts. She didn't want to fall into the trap of self-loathing again. She had tortured herself for months after the director left, wondering how she could have done something so stupid. Finally she had come to the conclusion that, in some cases, there was no blame. There were only actions and consequences.

Finally she continued. "After I was sick, I woke him up and told him to leave, that what we'd done was a mistake."

"Did he leave?" Michael was grateful that the man was nowhere around. It would have been pretty senseless to punch him out five years after the fact.

"Yes, he did," Dawn replied. "But for weeks afterward the man kept hassling me. He'd follow me into the forest, hang around the office after the others went home. No matter what I said or did he refused to leave me alone."

"What did you do?"

"The only thing I could think of. I contacted the board of directors and reported him."

"Let me guess. He promptly turned around and reported you."

Dawn nodded. "He claimed I'd seduced him with the intention of marriage. He even produced signed affidavits from his mother and a pile of other rich relatives, attesting to his sterling character. Can you imagine?"

"How did you manage to fight it?"

"Not on my own, that's for sure. You remember Jorge, the security guard? He and the other staff members got together and drew up a detailed report of this guy's behavior. They also produced a glowing account of the work I was doing at Montecristo. Because of their actions the case was sent to a tribunal for final judgment. That same day the director submitted his resignation."

"There were no repercussions?"

"None. He left, I stayed and that was the end of it. But I learned a lot about accountability, let me tell you."

"That's why you're worried about reporting Flavius."

Dawn nodded. "Most of the board members from five years ago are still there, and I know they would have fired me if it hadn't been for the tribunal. And even though I've proven myself through my work, I'm terrified of what might happen if I make waves again."

"I can understand. It's a tough situation."

Lost in thought, Dawn didn't hear. "If I go to the board about Flavius, he could lie, he could become violent. But on the other hand, I'm second in command. I have a responsibility toward the safety of the others. I can't just ignore the problem...."

Michael couldn't restrain himself any longer. He stood up and opened his arms. "Come here, honey."

She turned and looked at Michael, her eyes like those of a wounded doe—frightened, not daring to trust.

"Listen, baby, I'm not going to pressure you. You'll do what's right in the end. I know that."

It was too soon for Dawn to share his confidence, but she entered his embrace gladly. The tears she had tried to swallow now rose to engulf her, part of another lesson Dawn was still struggling to learn. She knew she was tough enough to cope with frustrations, injustices, all the cruel ironies of life. But one kind word, one tiny show of sympathy and she fell apart. It happened every time. It was happening now.

"CAN I ASK YOU a question, Dawn?"

It was Sunday morning, and they were in bed. Michael's hand lay gently on her breast, symbolic, it seemed, of the comfort they had finally found with each other after talking and loving far into the night.

"Of course, Michael. Ask me anything."

"Have you ever been to the waterfall with anyone else?"

Dawn knew, from the hesitation in his voice, how difficult it had been for him to ask. She was pleased that she could answer truthfully—and that Michael would know it was the truth. "I've never been to the waterfall with anyone but you."

He moaned and drew her closer. "That's good to hear."

She couldn't remember ever having been this open with a man. There had been moments, while she related the story of her former director, when she saw judgment in Michael's eyes. When that happened, she could barely meet his cold, flinty gaze. But Dawn continued, encouraged by some invisible source of strength, and eventually he revealed other emotions. Understanding, compassion, concern. All appeared in turn, and they were all part of Michael.

Then he told her of his own past—of the destructive, desperate years when he'd bridled against women, blaming them for his cold, uncaring wife. Dawn listened, fascinated, and realized that she had finally met a man who could accept her, totally, unconditionally—only because he had learned to accept himself.

But not even the night's wonderful revelations were enough to prevent reality from surfacing.

"I'll have to leave within the hour, Dawn."

She dug her nails into her palms, trying to deflect the rising anguish. "I know. When will you arrive in Winnipeg?"

"Around eleven tonight."

"That's a long day." Empty words, Dawn told herself. Why did they have to switch to empty words now, of all times?

"I wish you were coming," Michael said.

"I wish you were staying."

The stilted conversation was abandoned. Michael removed his hand upward from her breast. His fingers pressed into her shoulders. Wordlessly their mouths expressed the torture of farewell, the delight of reminiscence. Their tangled limbs and sweat-drenched bodies knew exactly how to recapture the magic...one last time.

When they finished making love, Michael groaned and fell away from her. "I can't believe this has happened."

"Neither can I. It's been so...sudden."

Not only sudden, but the culmination of so many variables. It began with a chance encounter in a seaside bar followed by a series of misunderstandings and near misses. And at the end, two days of joy. Not mere satisfaction or pleasure, but pure unadulterated joy.

"When do you think you'll come back?" Dawn asked.

"Probably in a month or two. It depends on my schedule."

"I see."

Thirty days, sixty days, the numbers didn't matter. Nothing would make this afternoon or tomorrow any easier to bear. Nothing—not even the admission of love—could alter the fact that Michael was leaving in less than an hour.

Abruptly Dawn sat up and swung her legs over the side. She wanted Michael to tell her he loved her. Somehow, she wanted these two days to become a lifetime.

But that was ludicrous, impossible. Michael hadn't said a word about love—or lifetimes. And because he hadn't, Dawn wanted him to leave. *Now.*

THEIR FINAL HOUR was strained. She went through the motions of preparing lunch, but neither one had much appetite or even the integrity to push their food away.

"I'll call you," Michael said when they were at the car.

"I don't have a phone, remember?"

He bit his lower lip, and his gaze fixed on hers as though he longed to say something, but couldn't. "That's right, I forgot. I'm afraid I'm not much of a letter writer."

Dawn was an avid correspondent, but she didn't admit it to Michael. What good would letters do? They were squiggles on a page, clever facsimiles of emotion that did nothing to keep a body warm at night. And if she wrote, and he didn't answer, she'd be all the lonelier. It wasn't worth the trouble.

"I'm not much for letters, either," she lied. "So just...uh, let me know when you'll be in the area again."

Dawn could have sworn Michael flinched. Maybe she'd sounded a little too cavalier. But maybe this was the best way, after all. Make it a clean cut. That way they could both heal more quickly.

His kiss was perfunctory, a peck on the lips that basically told her, "I can pretend not to care, too."

"Goodbye, Dawn."

"Goodbye, Michael." *I love you.* But, of course, Dawn didn't say those words. She simply watched as he got into the car and waved as he drove away.

She saw the flash of emerald an instant before Michael disappeared from view. Long, delicate wings, a scarlet breast and exquisite tail feathers, a rare quetzal bird was soaring low over the roof of Michael's car.

Biting her knuckle, Dawn choked back a sob. The sentiment might be touching, but the quetzal wasn't a portent of divine blessing. It was a bird.

Neither was Michael Garrett in any way heaven-sent. He was a man. Just a man. And he was gone.

8

MICHAEL RETURNED to the office Monday morning, jet-lagged and grumpy. He could have stayed in bed. He probably should have. But lying in bed reminded him of Dawn. So did showering and shaving and driving to work. No matter what he did, she was there—her beautiful shadowed image distracting, tantalizing. Michael couldn't stand it. He had to get her out of his head and make room for things that really mattered.

Not that he was discounting the time they'd spent together. It was spectacular, the best he'd ever known. But that was yesterday. Today he was facing a new week with a new set of priorities. And Michael made it a policy never to confuse his priorities.

He spent the morning reviewing the Agrofin file. Then, as usual, he consigned the client's problems to his subconscious and put the file away. Out of sight, out of mind. It was gone. In two months, when the time came to return to Costa Rica, Michael would know exactly how to handle the follow-up. That was the way his mind worked, and it had never let him down yet.

This time, however, there was a flaw. Dawn was supposed to have disappeared into the drawer along with the Agrofin file. She was, after all, part of Costa Rica. Part of yesterday. But it didn't happen.

By week's end she had managed to infiltrate his every waking moment—and most of the sleeping ones, too, Michael supposed. Everything he did, everything he saw was colored with the memory of Dawn, and it wasn't a pleasant experience. Okay, so maybe it was a little pleasant. But it was also disconcerting as hell.

Michael used to love watching women during lunch hour. The underground Concourse in downtown Winnipeg was ideal, teeming with good-looking, dressed-for-success females. He would buy himself a copy of the *Globe and Mail*, find a strategic spot in a glitzy café and enjoy.

It wasn't the same anymore. Sure, there were the same leather skirts, plunging necklines and the bodies to go with them, but nothing moved him the way it used to. Every woman Michael saw, no matter how stunning, he compared to Dawn. And to his amazement, Dawn invariably came up the winner.

He couldn't understand why. She was intriguing, certainly, and unlike any woman he'd ever met. But part of that could be attributed to the exotic setting of Montecristo. After all, how many women had their own private waterfall?

That didn't explain why he woke up every morning aroused, needing her. Not just any woman, but Dawn. It didn't explain why thoughts of her grew stronger every day, making work all but impossible, other women redundant. He couldn't go on like this. He had to do something to get Dawn out of his system.

Michael went home at the end of the week knowing there was only one thing left to do. He would have to pit Dawn against the Garrett Gauge of Minimum Requirements. A deluge of women after his divorce had induced Michael to set standards. If a woman didn't meet his three minimum requirements of beauty, brains and body, she wasn't worth his attention, period.

Eventually maturity and a gentler perception of women rendered Michael's standards obsolete, but maybe it was time to resurrect the gauge once more. Nothing else worked. This was his last resort.

He put on some mellow music, fixed himself a drink and sprawled across the sofa. "All right, Dawn," he said to the wall. "I didn't want to do this, but you've been driving me crazy. I have no choice. Either you pass the old Garrett Gauge, or out you go."

Number one, beauty.

Michael had to smile. He'd come a long way from his *Charlie's Angels* definition of good looks. Wiggles and jiggles still appealed, but somewhere along the line he'd learned to appreciate the subtler things. A woman's eyes, for example. Her smile. And the way she moved when she didn't think a man was looking.

Dawn passed—no, she excelled—on all those counts. Her beauty extended way beyond the normal standards. There was a radiance to her smile and her movements that reminded Michael of sunbeams. Of all the well-dressed women in the Concourse, there wasn't a sunbeam to be found.

Number two, brains.

This required more careful consideration. Michael hadn't dated a stupid woman in ten years, yet not all of them would have passed number two.

Working in the corporate world, he dealt regularly with female professionals—lawyers, accountants, entrepreneurs. For the most part, they were bright, self-motivated, successful. They belonged to the right country clubs, holidayed in the appropriate resorts and read the *Financial Post* cover to cover. Intelligent women, every one—and every one left him cold.

Now that he'd met Dawn, he understood why. Being a scientist, she was probably as well educated as any woman Michael had ever met. But Dawn didn't advertise her credentials. There were no initials behind her name, no diplomas on the walls. She was just a well-informed, well-adjusted woman who reflected a genuine zest for life. That kind of brilliance, in Michael's estimation, shone far longer than the textbook variety.

There could be no doubt that she passed number two. Number three, body.

Michael set his drink down and allowed his mind to wander. He'd forgotten how carefully he thought this one out. Maybe there had been a method to his madness after all.

His requirement was not that a woman possess a body like a *Playboy* centerfold, but that she love the body she possessed. That was a rare commodity in women. In combination with the first two, almost nonexistent.

Sex was important to Michael, almost as vital as breathing. Not only that, he *loved* it. He thoroughly enjoyed the erotic nuances of two bodies, naked and unashamed. Yet he'd never found a woman who consistently shared his enthusiasm.

He knew that women were supposed to enjoy making love as much as men. He also knew that for them it was largely an emotional experience, less dependent on the physical. And because Michael was a caring lover, he'd done his best to understand women's needs and to meet them.

His best never sufficed. Time and time again he staggered away from relationships disillusioned, frustrated. He finally came to the conclusion that a woman's interest in sex was directly proportionate to her self-esteem.

And there were very few women out there who liked themselves.

Dawn was an exception. She liked herself, and she liked sex. Not only the romantic words and soft kisses, but all the lust and energy and animal excitement that went along with lovemaking. Michael knew instinctively that Dawn would never manipulate or use sex as a form of reward and punishment. If a man were lucky enough to win her, she could truly be his helpmate, his partner, his forever love.

Michael had long since given up on finding such a woman. She had become a part of his fantasy life—a nameless, faceless female who loved him, but only in his dreams. Now, suddenly, there was a face to go along with the fantasy—a face, a body and a name. Dawn Avery.

So she'd passed the test. She was beautiful, intelligent, and she enjoyed making love. Had she failed, Michael might have eventually gotten her out of his head. Now he knew that would never happen. And now he had an even tougher problem—how to get Dawn Avery into his life . . . and persuade her to stay.

DAWN WAS WORKING LATE in the office Friday night. Exhausted, she had been up since sunrise, escorting a task force from the Ministry of Natural Resources through miles of muddy rain forest. Bad enough they had arrived unannounced, but the hours Dawn spent enlightening them would be a total waste of time. She knew the bureaucrats would present their findings to some nebulous committee, and the report would be filed somewhere and forgotten.

It would have been wise to go home, but Dawn wouldn't have slept. Whenever she climbed into bed these days, thoughts of Michael Garrett would intrude, and she'd toss and turn for hours. The first few nights the memory of him had been pleasing, like a romantic old movie one could watch over and over with delight.

But the delight eventually faded, and now she just missed Michael with an ache so profound and wearying that it frightened her. Even rest, when it finally came, provided no escape. Something would invariably waken Dawn during the heaviest part of sleep. A dream, a noise, she had no idea of the source. But it was powerful enough to make her sit bolt upright in bed with palms sweating, heart pounding.

Dawn would cry out, "Michael, where are you?"

But, of course, he wasn't there. Loneliness and desolation would sweep over her like a thick black cloud, and she would collapse, in tears, onto her pillow, only to struggle with sleep once again.

It wasn't worth the risk of going home. Not yet. Maybe if she stayed in the office long enough, fatigue would finally settle in. But in the meantime Dawn had plenty to keep her busy, even if she couldn't get Michael totally off her mind.

For weeks she'd been avoiding a stack of unanswered correspondence. There was the fourth-grader in Pennsylvania who wanted information on Montecristo for his science project. And then there was the grandmother from Utah who had "purchased" a hectare of the rain forest for her grandson's graduation and wanted a brochure to enclose with the card.

Trivial, perhaps, but at least the letters kept her hands and mind occupied. And she believed strongly in answering every piece of mail that came to Montecristo. In their efforts to expand the rain forest, they could hardly afford to be remote and unapproachable—a policy she had yet to impress upon Flavius.

The thought of him made her shudder. She and the director had had another row that afternoon while the bureaucrats were eating lunch in the village. It was her third argument with him that week, and the worst yet.

Flavius had come to her with a letter from an American electronics corporation, one of their major sponsors. "Electrocom has withdrawn their support of Montecristo," he said with typical gloom.

Dawn gulped her coffee and scalded her throat. "What? Let me see that!"

Several months earlier Electrocom had fallen victim to a hostile takeover by a large conglomerate. Dawn had business in San José at the time and advised Flavius by phone to contact the new executives and appeal for their continued support. The funds were critical, she had warned him, the equivalent of three months' salary for the entire staff.

The letter Flavius handed her now was a blanket cancellation of all philanthropic agreements entered into by Electrocom's former executives. "There's something odd about this," Dawn said. "They don't even acknowledge your letter."

"Hmmm, yes."

"Electrocom has supported Montecristo since the beginning. We were a major part of their advertising campaign. I can't imagine them just abandoning us."

Flavius hummed again. "It is unfortunate."

"You'd better write them another letter. Explain our situation and—"

"Why don't you write it?"

Dawn looked up. "Because you wrote the first one. It only makes sense."

"But you have a better command of the language."

"And you're the director, Flavius. You'll have more clout with the new executives. I'll take over the file after you've reestablished contact." She glanced across his desk. "Where is the folder, Flavius?"

"Uh, er . . . the folder?"

"The Electrocom file. Did you put it away?"

His basket was overflowing with paperwork. Dawn wouldn't have pried without his permission, but the Electrocom file was peeking from the bottom, so she pulled it out. Inside was an inch-high stack of correspondence, proof of the relationship Dawn had maintained meticulously for three years.

"Where's our copy?" she asked, flipping through the dossier.

"Copy?"

Dawn sighed and enunciated her words, as she often had to with Flavius. "Where is the copy of your letter to Electrocom? Didn't you make a carbon?"

"I . . . I don't know. I don't recall."

There were times when Flavius truly didn't understand what was going on. Other times, he did and tried to cover up. Dawn was learning to recognize the difference. "Don't tell me you never wrote to them," she said.

"Certainly, I did."

"Then why isn't the letter on file?"

"It's . . . uh, I don't know." His bony hands fluttered through the air. "You really should not annoy me with such questions. I have a journal to complete, and besides I am your director, not your stenographer."

Dawn's reaction wasn't gracious. Her nerves already frayed, she shrieked at Flavius, "Don't try to impress me with your title, Doctor Van der Pol! That might work in your pretentious European labs, but not around here."

He squared his shoulders, as though to deflect her criticism. "If Electrocom was so important to you, why did you not handle the situation yourself?"

"I was in San José, remember? I read about the takeover in the paper, and I didn't have a typewriter or their address. So I phoned you. If you recall, Flavius, you did agree to contact them. But obviously there are no guarantees attached to your agreements!"

They battled back and forth for several minutes, but the argument went nowhere. Flavius snatched up his journal, stormed out of the office and locked himself in his cabin for the rest of the day.

Dawn, meanwhile, placed a call that she should have made a week ago to San José. There was no more time to lose. If something wasn't done about their finances, salaries would go unpaid. And if something wasn't done about Flavius, worse things could happen.

Dr. Bustamante, a hospital administrator, was chairman of the board for Montecristo. When Dawn identified herself, he immediately became aloof. It wasn't a good sign. Dawn remembered all too well that he'd been a staunch ally of her first director and would have had her fired if not for the support of her colleagues.

After a few strained minutes of small talk, he asked, "What can I do for you, Doctor Avery?"

The chairman was one of the few people who called her by her title, but he did so with the faintest note of condescension.

"One of our major sponsors has gone into receivership."

To her surprise, Dr. Bustamante proved sympathetic about the money and promised to arrange for emergency funds at once. He was less amenable, however, when Dawn outlined the problems they were encountering with Flavius Van der Pol.

"These are serious accusations you are making, Doctor Avery."

"It's a serious situation," she replied.

"Flavius Van der Pol is a brilliant scientist. He came to us highly recommended."

"I am not challenging his merits as a scientist, Doctor Bustamante, but I don't believe Flavius can adapt to the life-style in Montecristo."

"Perhaps he requires more time. He has only been there several months."

"I hoped so, too, at first. But he's getting worse instead of better. Because of him everyone is tense and short-tempered. Half our volunteers are refusing to come to work anymore." Dawn paused long enough to control the desperation in her voice. "I'm convinced that Flavius requires professional help, Doctor. I don't think there's anything we can do for him here."

At last she wore down the chairman's defenses. "Very well, Doctor Avery, send me a detailed report on Flavius's behavior. I shall study the matter and, if necessary, introduce it at our next board meeting."

"When's that?"

"In two weeks."

"Two weeks?" Dawn shrilled. "Couldn't you call an emergency meeting?"

"Certainly I could, if the situation were an emergency. What I perceive, however, is a simple clash of personalities. And, in your case, this is not the first time it's happened. Isn't that right, Doctor?"

"You . . . you actually think I'm responsible?" she stammered, numb with disbelief.

"I can only consider the facts. During the time you have been in Montecristo, we have hired how many— four directors? None of them have worked out. Surely that gives you some indication of where the true problem lies."

He actually did think this was her fault!

"But two of the directors were excellent," Dawn argued. "They only quit because they found better postings elsewhere."

"Which makes one wonder why they were driven to take those other postings."

Dawn bit her tongue. Otherwise she would have apprised Dr. Bustamante, loudly, of the real reason directors never stayed in Montecristo. It was a lousy job with high accountability and few rewards. They had a shoestring operating budget, no running water or electricity in their homes—and, obviously, a board of directors that couldn't care less.

But Dawn's emotions were too close to the surface. She didn't trust herself to speak without offending him further and risking her own position. So she muttered a few inconsequential words, managed a civil goodbye and slammed the receiver down.

Why the hell did she bother? And why was she so worried about her job? It would serve the board right if she just up and quit. Let the developers buy Montecristo and turn it into one huge cow pasture. In twenty years Costa Rica would be a desert, and no one could say she hadn't warned them.

People claimed to care; they made the right noises. But Dawn was having trouble believing that these days. Poor people who lived in the vicinity considered the rain forest a threat to their meager landholdings. The urban rich enjoyed the laurels heaped on them for supporting a cause. And the corporations saw Montecristo as a tax write-off. There wasn't a genuine ally to be found anywhere.

Incongruously Dawn thought of Michael. He was different. He wasn't a supporter or a foe of Montecristo, yet he really did seem to care. When Dawn shared her problems with him, he listened closely and he understood.

It had to be a special talent of Michael's. She had never met anyone who could empathize as he could. Apart from being a wonderful lover, he took the time to make her feel worthwhile, important, unique. They were qualities Dawn knew she possessed, but in the day-to-day struggle of preserving Montecristo, they must have gotten buried somewhere.

The night she met him, Michael had referred to Dawn as one lone voice crying in the wilderness. His perception of her, even then, was uncanny. That's exactly how she was feeling tonight. Like one lone voice in the middle of nowhere . . . and nobody was listening.

Dawn awoke to a jangling noise. She sat up, bleary-eyed. This wasn't her bed. This was the office, and the phone was ringing.

Rubbing her eyes, she picked up the receiver. *"Buenas noches, Montecristo."*

"Could I speak to Dawn Avery, please?"

"Speaking."

"This is Michael Garrett."

Her sleepy eyes sprang open. "Michael? Is that really you?"

He laughed gently. "Yes, it really is. How are you, Dawn?"

She had to be dreaming. Nothing this wonderful could possibly be happening. Only the kink in her neck was evidence of reality. Dawn rubbed her neck and tried to sound coherent. "I'm, uh . . . fine, I mean . . . well, things are pretty awful, but—never mind about that. How are you?"

"I'm okay. I can't believe I was lucky enough to catch you on a Friday night."

"I had a lot of work to finish up." Dawn's cheeks flushed when she remembered that Michael, and not work, was the real reason she'd stayed late. "Are you coming back to Costa Rica sooner than planned?"

"No, I won't be able to swing it before mid-June at the earliest."

"But that's two months from now," she said, desolation threatening once again.

"I know, and I can't wait that long to see you again."

At least he *wanted* to see her, Dawn reasoned, even if he couldn't. "I've missed you, too," she admitted. "Montecristo hasn't felt the same since your visit."

"That surprises me."

"Why?"

"You were pretty cool the day I left. I figured you'd forget me the instant I was gone."

"Oh, no, I would never forget you." Dawn struggled to recapture the emotions of that dismal Sunday afternoon. When she realized how callous she must have seemed, Dawn felt terrible. "I didn't mean to be distant."

"What were you trying to be?"

"I guess. . . I just didn't want to admit how much it hurt seeing you go."

"Would it have hurt more to tell me?"

Dawn drew in a sharp breath, startled by his candor. "If I'd told you, could you have stayed longer?"

"You know I couldn't."

"So now you understand why I didn't say anything. You didn't need the pressure."

Michael didn't answer. Dawn wondered whether she had ruined things with her glib tongue. Except, this time, she wasn't being glib. "Are you still there?" she finally ventured.

"Yes. I was just recalling how cold we were with each other at the end. I tried to tell myself you didn't matter and that I'd be able to forget you in no time."

"Did you forget me?" she asked, realizing too late it was a stupid question.

"Would I be calling you if I had?"

"Probably not. So why did you call?"

"I wanted to invite you to Canada."

Her mouth dropped. "I beg your pardon?"

"Before you say no, hear me out. I've juggled my schedule so I can take a week off. But there's a half-day seminar in the middle that I can't cancel. Otherwise, I'd have come to Costa Rica to see you."

Dawn's emotions went into a tailspin. To think that Michael would have come all this way just to visit—not even on business! Suddenly the foolish pride she'd exhibited last week felt even more foolish. "You'd like me to spend a whole week with you?"

"Even longer if you'd like. I can wire the tickets to San José. All I need is for you to say yes."

Yes, Michael, of course I'll come to Canada! I'd go anywhere for you anytime! But that was just wishful thinking, and life wasn't made of wishes. "When would you want me to come?" she asked cautiously.

"Next Friday."

Her heart stopped. That was only a week from now. In seven days she could actually be with Michael. In his arms, loving him . . .

But it was preposterous, unthinkable. With all the things that were happening, she could never get away that quickly. Flavius was going off the deep end. They were desperately short of money. Montecristo's staff was quitting. She would need at least . . .

Dawn glanced around the office. At least what? How long would she need to extricate herself from this place? A month? A year? An eternity?

"Are you still there, Dawn?"

"Yes. Yes, I'm still here." It would take an eternity.

"Is there any chance you can get away? I know it's short notice . . ."

Tears pooled at the corners of Dawn's eyes. She had never felt so trapped, helpless and overjoyed all at once. "I don't know, Michael. I'm grateful for the invitation, but I'm not sure I could make arrangements in time."

"I understand. If you could tell me your final decision by Tuesday, I could still get the tickets to you on time."

Michael's hopefulness was touching. Dawn felt terrible having to turn him down. But she had to. The rain forest was her life; she had a responsibility to this place. Yet, while Dawn was busy arguing with herself, she could feel her grip on Montecristo loosening.

Michael wasn't talking about a lifetime away. Only seven days. So what was the worst that could happen if she abandoned Montecristo for a week? Her paperwork was caught up. Dr. Bustamante had promised to look after salaries. As for Flavius, he would be forced to look after Montecristo on his own. That wasn't a reassuring thought, but what real harm could he do? If there was an emergency, Jorge could handle it.

Her resolve firm, Dawn said, "There's no need to wait until Tuesday. I've decided to take you up on the offer, Michael. And I can't wait to see you!"

9

MICHAEL WAITED at the foot of the escalator in Winnipeg's International Airport. The flight from Miami had been announced ten minutes ago. Most of the passengers had already descended and were making their way toward the baggage carousel.

He jammed his hands into the pockets of his suede jacket, willing himself to calm down. There was still no sign of Dawn, but it was too soon to begin serious worrying. After all, someone had to be the last passenger off the plane. No reason why it couldn't be her.

When ten minutes dragged into fifteen, then twenty, it was time to worry. There were only a few stragglers coming down the stairs now, and Dawn wasn't one of them.

She must have missed the Miami connection. He knew she had a two-hour layover, but if they were late taking off from San José, that might not have been enough time. Then again, maybe she'd never caught the flight from San José. The road might have washed out in Montecristo. Dawn could still be stuck somewhere on that mountain.

He shouldn't have left the house so early. Michael had arrived at the airport two hours ahead of time, just in case, but that was stupid. Dawn might have tried phoning, and he wasn't there. Even if she'd left a message, his remote was at home in the briefcase. There was no way of checking his messages from here.

Pacing the terminal, Michael tried to get a grip on himself. He'd done so well counting down the days, hours and minutes until her arrival. But he'd run out of patience. He and Dawn only had a week together. From now on every minute without her was a minute lost.

He was just about to look for an airline representative when he saw her. Dawn, coming down the glass-walled corridor on the second floor. But she was moving at a snail's pace. Any slower and she'd be going backward. What the heck was the matter with her? Was she sick?

Then he realized she wasn't alone. Dawn was accompanied by an elderly couple. The woman had an arm linked around her husband's, while the man walked with a cane. That would explain Dawn's pace. She was also engaged in intense conversation, which would explain why she wasn't looking for him.

Michael felt a twinge of resentment. He had been pacing this blasted terminal for two hours, waiting for her. The least she could do was show a little interest and look for him, for Pete's sake.

Angrily he pushed the thought aside. What right did he have to dictate Dawn's behavior? She was, by nature, outgoing and friendly. It was one of the many things he loved about her. And if he weren't so damn uptight, he'd be pleased that she was enjoying herself.

The glass doors slid open, and Dawn, a winter coat slung over her arm, stepped onto the escalator. She and her two elderly friends descended as though it were the continuation of a private party. The couple seemed thoroughly engrossed in what Dawn had to say, and she appeared to thrive on their attention. Laughing, gesturing, she was as animated as she'd been that first night Michael had seen her in the Costa Rican bar.

Meanwhile, he had the rare opportunity to admire her, unnoticed. Dawn looked fabulous. Her dress was made from some thin cottony fabric, a jungle print in rust, olive and gold. Her waist was cinched with a wide belt, and her hair fell in chestnut curls across her shoulders. But the pièce de résistance was a floppy-brimmed leather hat that shaded her eyes and accentuated her elegant stature. Not many women could have pulled it off, but Dawn wore the hat with panache. Despite his agitation, Michael couldn't have been prouder.

Finally she turned around and saw him. "Michael!" she cried out, waving.

He smiled.

Dawn stepped off the escalator, but she didn't come right away. She waited to help the couple off and pointed them toward the baggage area. Then, holding her hat, she ran to Michael.

He thought his heart would burst. She was here! She had actually come to Canada to be with him. A few seconds later Dawn was in his arms.

"Oh, Michael, I am so happy to see you! I had the most wonderful flight. This is the nicest thing anyone has ever done for me."

"You deserve it, honey, and I'm so glad you're here. Do you ever look gorgeous."

"So do you," she murmured, lifting her mouth eagerly to his.

Dawn's kisses were exuberant—wet, happy greetings that made Michael laugh—and nearly made him cry. When her hat fell off amid all the excitement, he caught it in the vicinity of her bottom. What a convenient excuse to press himself to her, as he'd been aching to do for weeks.

Neither one cared that they were in an airport full of people. Neither one noticed that their embraces were bordering on intimate. As far as Michael was concerned, they'd been apart too long. It was bound to show.

He couldn't get enough of her. Dawn's shape, her scent, the beating of her heart, the sound of her laughter. Everything about the woman seemed custom-made to drive him wild.

It was Dawn who finally pulled away, laughing and breathless. "Wow, I've never had a welcome like this before!"

Michael grinned and kept his arms looped lightly around her waist. "You've never been to Winnipeg. We're friendly around here."

"No kidding? I could really get to like this place."

Please do, Dawn. Please like Winnipeg. But it was too soon to make such requests aloud. It was even too soon to hope that she would. After a week of togetherness, Michael might be happy to see her on the plane to Costa Rica. Not that this was a test. But when it came to women, this wouldn't be the first time he misjudged a situation.

Now, however, as he gazed into sparkling green eyes, Michael couldn't imagine being wrong. He couldn't imagine wanting a woman as much as Dawn—and then changing his mind. If the agony of waiting had been any indication, seeing her leave would be sheer hell.

But hell was a week away. He didn't intend to rush it.

"I met the sweetest couple on the plane," Dawn was saying as Michael led her to the baggage carousel. "They're in their eighties and still so much in love. It's amazing."

"That is pretty rare. What's their secret?"

"I wish I knew. They just came back from the Yucatán. They live in Winnipeg but spend every winter someplace warm."

"They seemed to enjoy your company."

"I was enjoying theirs. We chatted all the way from Miami. We talked about where I live, and as it turns out, they've wanted to visit Costa Rica for years. Now they're actually considering coming next winter."

Michael grinned. "Good for you."

He had forgotten that when Dawn was excited she talked in one nonstop sentence. He had also forgotten how charming she was while doing it.

"I told them if they came to Montecristo, I'd be happy to give them a tour."

He looked at her teasingly. "You're not giving them the same tour you gave me."

First Dawn stared at him. Then she laughed and blushed. "No, Michael. No one gets the tour that I gave you."

DAWN WOULD NEVER have believed that being with Michael again could be this easy. The conversation in the car flowed as though they had been friends forever, catching up on years instead of weeks. The topics were hardly earthshaking, ranging from the weather in Manitoba to anecdotes about Costa Rica. But the words didn't matter. Feelings did, and Dawn hadn't felt such feelings in years.

"Do you remember Marisa and Enrique?" she asked, admiring Michael's profile. His chin was so strong, the length of his nose just perfect.

"How could I forget? That was the night we met."

"Oh, right. They had a baby boy who weighed eight pounds, six ounces. They called him Alejandro Manuel Inocencia . . . something, something. I forget the rest."

Michael laughed. "Big handle for a little guy."

"Isn't it, though?" Dawn noticed that he still wore the same cologne. It was a subtle, complex scent that had lingered on her pillowcase for days. She remembered feeling desolate when it finally disappeared.

"How is the family?" Michael asked. "Are they doing okay?"

"As far as I know. I've only spoken to Lito, Marisa's father, on the phone, but I'm hoping I'll get the chance to visit soon."

"I'll bet he's a proud grandpa."

"Oh, yes. He's convinced Alejandro will be president of Costa Rica one day."

Michael laughed again. "Maybe he will. Who knows?"

Now Dawn remembered how much she had enjoyed the sound of his laughter. Strangely enough, he was better looking than she remembered, too. In her memory Michael was tall, strong-featured and masculine, but beyond that she couldn't quite capture him. During their brief interlude in Costa Rica, there hadn't been enough time to gather details and commit them to memory.

These past few weeks, whenever she closed her eyes and visualized the man, only the subtler details came into focus. The texture of his skin, taste of his lips, the sound of Michael's voice when he whispered her name. Those were the images that lingered, that made her clutch his pillow every night to fall asleep.

The sudden blending of memories and the current reality of Michael was almost overwhelming. Dawn hadn't realized it, but time had already begun to seep through the memories, muting the shades of their passion to a tender bittersweet. If she'd never seen him again, she might have learned to live with it.

Not anymore. Seeing Michael again brought everything back in blinding, brilliant Technicolor. She knew now why they'd become lovers, why resisting him had been virtually impossible. Dawn also knew that she would never forget what he looked like again.

Michael lived in a high-rise condominium overlooking a park with a river. The Assiniboine, he'd called it— one of several rivers that meandered through the city. The park was apparently one of Winnipeg's loveliest, but it was dark by the time they pulled into the parking garage, so Dawn would have to wait until morning to appreciate it.

The building, however, was impressive. The lobby had luxurious marble floors and a central fountain. The waiting area featured tropical plants and furniture upholstered in plum-colored velvet.

"Good grief!" Dawn exclaimed, taking in everything as Michael led her to the elevator. "You must do awfully well in loss control."

"It's just a lobby," he said. "It's not as though I spend a lot of time down here."

Michael's modesty impressed her. He dressed expensively; the suede jacket alone represented three months' salary for Dawn. But he had a way of making his success seem irrelevant, reminding her of an old adage: elegance was born and not made.

"Welcome home," he said, opening the door to his penthouse apartment.

"Good grief!" Dawn said again, stepping inside.

After a kiss that made her heart flutter, Michael gestured toward the living room. "Make yourself at home.

I'll just take your bags into the bedroom, and I'll be right out."

She felt a twinge of panic when he left, then mustered the nerve to enter his living room. Maybe she was used to the snug confines of her cabin, but she couldn't imagine ever feeling at home in a place like this.

The rooms sprawled on forever with floor-to-ceiling windows, oak floors and gleaming brass fixtures. One wall contained a huge television screen and what appeared to be state-of-the-art stereo and video equipment. There was a white stone fireplace with an area rug and a built-in corner bar with a full collection of liquor that looked untouched. The dining room furniture was brass and glass. The living room was leather with a chocolate-brown sofa and chairs that epitomized the successful single male.

Dawn wandered agog into the kitchen, a fluorescent room of white on white, and did what she usually did in new kitchens. She turned on the taps. There it was, all right. Hot and cold running water. When a person lived without basics, it was always the basics that mattered most. Satisfied with the water, Dawn turned her attention to the built-in appliances.

"Do you think you'll be comfortable here for a week?" came a voice from behind.

Michael slipped his arms around her waist, and she leaned into his embrace, marveling at the way their contours fit. "Where—in the kitchen?" she teased.

"Are you kidding? I'd never do that, at least for the first few days. I meant the apartment in general."

Dawn turned to look at him. An innocent enough gesture, but the effect was incredible. Her buttocks rubbed against his lower parts, and her breasts grazed his chest. By the time they were facing each other, both had been aroused by the erotic friction. "Your place is fascinating, Michael, and so are you. But it'll take me a week just to find my way around."

He smiled and cradled her face. "Don't worry, baby. I'll make sure you don't get lost."

"That's a relief."

"I still can't believe you're here."

"Neither can I."

"I've been going nuts waiting for this day to arrive, and I was so afraid something would go wrong."

"What could possibly go wrong?" she asked, basking in his warmth, wishing he would kiss her.

"I don't know. Montecristo could have fallen off the map, or you might have changed your mind."

"I would never change my mind."

"Thank God, because I'm not sure I could have handled that."

Dawn was suddenly reminded of another attribute— Michael's openness. So few men could admit to their vulnerability, as if doing so would make them less of a man. In Dawn's opinion they were wrong.

"I've been so excited about this trip," she said. "I had to keep pinching myself to believe it was happening."

"I'm glad I could do that for you."

Dawn's most recent wish came true when Michael lowered his face and kissed her. His kisses, she decided, were superb, every one individually colored for the occasion. The exhilaration she had felt at the airport was now replaced by a deeper emotion, a simmering hunger that burned hot wherever she and Michael were touching.

Suddenly mouths weren't enough. Dawn moved her body closer, pressing herself to him. Neither could hands do justice to the need inside. Thighs intertwined, they rubbed together slowly, acknowledging the mutual flame and stoking it.

Their passion rose so fast and so furious that Michael could have taken her right there. Dawn knew it instinctively, and part of her wanted him to. In a matter of minutes their passion could have been assuaged. But this reunion was too special to be rushed. She hoped Michael would feel the same way.

He must have sensed her pulling back. Michael loosened his embrace and held her at a safe distance by the shoulders. "My goodness, woman, I'd almost forgotten the hair-trigger effect you have on me."

Knowing they were on safer ground, Dawn grinned at him flirtatiously. "You have the same effect on me, you know."

"I do?"

At first Dawn didn't answer. She assumed he was fishing for a compliment. But she could see from his eyes that he wasn't, and that amazed her. Michael Garrett had literally everything going for him. That he would doubt his effect on a woman was astonishing. That he would question it aloud, even more so.

"Mr. Garrett," she said, running her hands along his chest. "Let me set the record straight. I have wanted you—no, I have *ached* for you ever since you left my bed in Montecristo."

Michael's eyes warmed with appreciation. That was when Dawn knew she had said the right thing.

"We're not going to rush this," he said. "You've come all the way to Canada to see me, so I'm going to make sure we do it right."

Dawn grinned. "Sounds great."

It was just as well they hadn't given in to temptation. The doorbell rang. Dawn jumped at the sound, then realized with chagrin that she hadn't heard a doorbell in years.

"Just what we need," Michael griped, stalking from the kitchen. "Company."

Dawn suddenly felt glued to the floor. What if it was a group of his civilized corporate friends—or even worse, some blond-bombshell neighbor pretending to borrow sugar to catch a glimpse of Michael's latest conquest? Maybe it was naive of her, but Dawn had never envisioned his friends, nor anticipated meeting them. Not that she couldn't handle it. But tonight?

"Dawn, there's someone here to see you!"

Her jaw dropped. This had to be some kind of practical joke. She didn't know a soul in Canada. And if this was a practical joke, heaven help her. She couldn't imagine a week of whoopee cushions and sneezing powder.

"I'll, uh . . . I'll be right there," she said, realizing she couldn't postpone the inevitable.

The walk from the kitchen to the front hall took forever. A woman was standing in the doorway, smiling. But she wasn't the blond bombshell Dawn had envisioned. She was kind of plain and dressed like a bellhop, of all things.

"Are you Dawn Avery?" she asked.

"Yes."

"This is for you." She reached behind the door and slid out a giant gift-wrapped box that stood over five feet high.

"Wh-what is this?" Dawn asked, glancing at Michael.

"Who knows," he said, grinning like a Cheshire cat. "Guess it's up to you to find out."

The bellhop lady brought the box into the apartment, then tipped her hat and said goodbye. Michael shut the door behind her.

An odd mixture of emotions bubbled inside Dawn as she stared at the parcel with the huge purple bow. She felt suspicious, excited, flattered and incredulous. She might have stood there, emoting forever, if Michael hadn't asked, "Were you planning to open it eventually?"

"Oh, yes. Yes, of course." She untied the bow and found a card underneath, which she opened and read aloud. "To Dawn. Welcome to Canada. Love, Michael."

She looked up at him, wide-eyed. *Love, Michael?* He was looking at her in a way that suggested he meant every word. So maybe he did. "Thank you," she whispered.

"You're welcome." He motioned toward the parcel. "You're not finished yet."

She ripped off the paper, feeling like a little girl on Christmas morning. Then, carefully, she lifted the lid, and a bunch of silver spheres floated from the box.

"Balloons!" she cried.

There were a dozen helium balloons tied with multicolored ribbons, and every one bore a message. Some said, To a Special Lady, from Her Secret Admirer. Others were emblazoned with today's date, the day they'd met, and several had pictures painted on them—a couple dancing, palm trees, a secluded waterfall.

Dawn watched the balloons sail around the room and, for the first time in her life, was totally speechless. No words could possibly have expressed her feelings. Her eyes brimming, she went to Michael and threw her arms around his neck.

She hugged him for a long while, alternately sniffling and laughing with delight. "No one has ever . . . I don't know what to . . . oh, Michael, you really are the sweetest man!"

He tangled his fingers in her hair and held her close, tacit reassurance that words weren't necessary. "I'm glad you like them, honey."

"Like them? I love them!" *I love you.* She nearly said the words aloud, but the time wasn't right. She knew it would be soon, though, very soon.

"Now," he said, tipping his head back to look at her, "what would you like to do about dinner?"

"Dinner?" she gasped, as if food were just one more incredible surprise.

"It's not a big deal," he said, picking up on her mood. "I usually have dinner every day around this time."

"But I ate on the plane," she said.

He draped an arm around her shoulders and led her to the sofa. "Airplane food doesn't count. So how about I list the choices, and you can decide."

"Okay." A woman could get to like all of this attention. She had better be careful.

"I've made reservations at a restaurant, but if you're tired, we can cancel them. There's steak and crab legs in the fridge and the makings for my special Caesar salad."

"Steak and crab legs?" Dawn sank—forever, it seemed—into Michael's leather sofa. "Good heavens, I'd forgotten such decadent food existed."

Michael sank beside her. "You've been in the jungle too long. That's why it's good to get out once in a while."

"I'm beginning to realize that. I love steak and crab legs—and Caesar salad's my favorite. But you know what I'd really like?"

"Tell me."

"Promise you won't laugh?"

"Cross my heart."

As it turned out, Michael broke his promise, but because he had indulged her, Dawn forgave him. An hour later they were sitting in front of the fireplace with an extra large pizza, double cheese, and a bottle of French burgundy.

"You can't imagine," Dawn said, tugging at a string of mozzarella on her plate, "what it's like to have a pizza craving in Montecristo at midnight."

"It must be rough." Michael served Dawn another gooey slice and one for himself.

"It is. My theory is, if heaven exists, it'll have to have a ready supply of pizza, double cheese. Otherwise, why call it heaven?"

Michael threw back his head and laughed. "You really are enjoying this, aren't you?"

Dawn's eyes widened. "Yes. Aren't you?"

"Oh, honey, don't get me wrong. Sharing a pizza with you is terrific. I just want your first night in Canada to be special."

Dawn looked up at the silver spheres floating around them and the twinkle of city lights far below. Then she looked at the man who'd made it all happen. "Michael, you have got to know that this is the most special night of my life."

10

DAWN CAME TO HIM sometime after midnight. Michael was already in bed, lying on his side, a lamp glowing softly behind him. She had undressed in the bathroom, not out of modesty, but to prepare herself with extra care.

In San José, a few hours before her flight, Dawn had splurged on perfume and a midnight-blue teddy of satin and lace. She was wearing them now, entering the bedroom with the confidence of a woman about to be loved.

The lingerie was cut high at the hips, low at the breasts. Jasmine and sandalwood enveloped Dawn in gentle, curling wisps. She hoped Michael would enjoy the scent, enjoy her.

His expression told her all she needed to know for now. Awed, wonderstruck, Michael gazed at Dawn as though she was his first woman. Smiling tremulously, he threw back the covers, inviting her wordlessly to join him. At that instant Dawn caught a glimpse of his nakedness and felt his emotions mirrored. Michael could have been, for all the world, her first man.

Strangely there was no urgency this time, none of the fumbled groping they had experienced in the kitchen. That, too, pleased Dawn. She intended to spend all night loving Michael. There was no need to rush. And she sensed, happily, that he intended the same thing.

"You're breathtaking," he murmured, taking her into his arms and holding her.

Dawn gasped and closed her eyes, focusing on the perfection of their bodies aligned. Everything met exactly where it should—arousing, sensitizing, filling the bedroom with erotic expectation. "So are you, Michael."

"It sounds incredible," he said, his hands wandering along her back, "but I have fantasies about you in dark blue lace."

"Really?" She brought her lips to his earlobe and nipped gently. "Do I match the fantasy?"

"The fantasy doesn't even come close to the real thing."

The fit of his hands around her breasts was flawless. When he rasped the sensitive flesh with his thumbs, Dawn arched back, moaning his name, needing him. Michael responded by taking a nipple in his mouth and stimulating it to rosy hardness. Then, to her amazement, he drew her entire breast into his mouth.

She gasped in sheer delight. Had her breasts been fuller, the feat would have been impossible. For the first time in her life she had cause to revel in their modest dimensions.

The feelings Michael invoked while suckling were complex. Dawn felt totally absorbed, totally surrounded by his passion. At the same time she felt an awakening, as though her anatomy had always known such love was possible—and had merely been waiting for the right lover to show her.

He lavished both breasts thoroughly and, with his hand, sought the deeper heat between her legs. "Oh, that feels beautiful," she whispered, astonished by the lightning intensity of his touch.

Dawn had been moist for hours, aroused by Michael's very nearness. Now, as his fingers plied the dampness, Dawn felt proud of her body's response. She wanted him. And she also wanted Michael to know how much.

He was the kind of lover, Dawn had discovered, who sacrificed his own pleasure for the sake of his partner. Perhaps she recognized it because she was the same way herself—so intent on giving that receiving was sometimes overlooked. With a selfish lover, one never received at all.

Dawn would never allow that to happen with Michael. She urged him onto his back, opened his legs and positioned herself between them. Then she took him into her mouth... and she gave.

Michael, to her delight, wasn't shy. He tucked both pillows under his head and watched, spellbound, as Dawn worked her magic. Sometimes, however, he couldn't watch. The passion would be too much, and he would squeeze his eyes shut, upper body thrashing.

"Oh, Dawn, I have never..." he would cry. "Never felt anything so... beautiful in my life."

"It's for you, darling," she whispered, "so enjoy..."

Dawn caressed him with her fingertips, then lowered her mouth again, flicking her tongue against the most delicate parts. Her skill wasn't so much learned as instinctive. She could tell by Michael's reactions what pleased him most, what drove him over the brink and beyond. And with some deep, inner wisdom she knew how to bring him back before he lost control, thereby prolonging and enhancing his pleasure.

Finally she drew Michael into her mouth as deeply as she could and hummed. Somewhere in her collection of erotica she had read that the vibrations of a woman's vocal cords were like magic on a man. With the most sensitive part of him against her palate, Dawn hummed a low tone, then slowly worked her way up the scale.

His response was explosive. Michael cried out, and his fingers curled into the mattress. He begged Dawn not to stop and pleaded that she would. It was, she suspected, too much, not enough—and more than he had ever dreamed of.

At precisely the right moment she released him from her sorcery and rolled onto her back. Michael entered her at once, thrusting deeply, bringing Dawn to an urgent, fevered pitch. Then he surprised her with a skill of his own. He withdrew suddenly and, before Dawn could protest, sat back on his knees and loved her with his mouth.

His tongue found the tiny bud, already heated and swollen. His touch, applied with such care, sent Dawn soaring. Now she understood how Michael felt when she pleasured him. Lost, uncontrolled, flying through frequencies almost too high to be endured.

Thinking she would faint, she pleaded with Michael. "It's too much, please..." But when he withdrew she pleaded again, "Don't stop...don't ever stop."

They loved, it seemed, forever. Again and again Michael thrust himself inside her, bringing Dawn to the crest of repletion, only to withdraw, excite her in his other way and lift her to a higher repletion. Dawn had never in her life been so erotically ministered, so completely loved.

At the end he was inside her. A fireburst, as infinite as the universe, enveloped them both. Dawn clung to Michael, his body drenched with sweat and tears, their fluids mingled as deeply as their souls.

It was nearly sunrise when they finally fell asleep. Wrapped in each other's arms, Dawn and Michael knew instinctively that when they awoke their lives would never be the same again.

DAWN STOOD at the bedroom door, watching Michael sleep. She would have loved to wake him and make love before they began their first day together. But he looked so peaceful lying there, hands tucked under his pillow, covers tangled around his legs.

She closed the door quietly and went down the hall to the living room. The place looked different in daylight, stark and remote, like an insecure woman caught without her makeup.

Dawn crossed the room and pulled back the drapes. That was better. Sunlight flooded through the glass doors, warming and softening the contours of the room.

She would have loved to stroll outside, but being on the top floor, there was no yard, only a balcony—a cold slab of concrete and railing that jutted into space. Far below was the park Michael had talked about—a rolling landscape of river and trees that was probably delightful in the summer. But it was only May, and May in Manitoba was nothing like the tropics. There was still snow on the ground, ice on the river, and the hardwoods had only begun to bud.

Dawn shivered and turned away, grateful for the sunshine and Michael. She didn't care if they had blizzards for a week, as long as she could stay indoors and be loved the way she had been last night.

Michael deserved a big breakfast. Heaven knows he had burned enough calories. Humming to herself, Dawn padded into the kitchen. She looked forward to doing things for her lover, and over the next week she intended to do all she could.

Apparently Michael had pampering in mind, as well. The refrigerator was stocked with all sorts of gourmet delights—Italian sausage, kippered herring, Brie—and exotic condiments Dawn had never heard of. If she wasn't careful, this sophisticated life-style could spoil her. Then again, what a blissful way to be spoiled.

After rummaging for a while, she found eggs, scallions and fresh bell peppers, the perfect ingredients for *huevos rancheros*. Michael enjoyed spicy food, so he would probably like them.

Fifteen minutes later Dawn had all but given up on making breakfast. She couldn't find a cutting board, there were no burners on the stove and the other appliances were equally inoperable. Since when had kitchens become so complicated?

The only thing Dawn could do, while waiting for Michael, was to plug in the kettle. She was hunting down tea bags, grumbling to herself, when he found her.

"Good morning, beautiful."

With her head stuck deep in a cupboard, Dawn started. She backed out carefully and stood up. "Good morning," she said with a sheepish smile. "I'm not hiding, really. I was going to surprise you with breakfast."

"That's nice of you." Michael had just come out of the shower and was wearing nothing but a towel around his waist. He looked clean, well rested and dangerously virile.

"The problem is," she continued, her eyes feasting, "I don't know how to operate any of your appliances. I feel like I'm in the control center at NASA."

He tousled her hair lovingly. "Poor thing, I'll have to give you a crash course. But first, let me hold you."

Michael opened his arms, and Dawn moved eagerly into his embrace. He smelled of soap and himself—a delicious, subtle scent she recalled from the night before. The memories it evoked were almost powerful enough to drive her back to bed and forget breakfast altogether. But it would be wise to eat something first.

"Did you sleep well?" she asked, planting tiny kisses along his collarbone.

"Like a baby," he replied, sliding his hips rhythmically against hers. "How about you?"

"Uh-huh." Maybe a quick bite of toast would be enough, she reasoned. They could always eat later.

"I missed you," Michael said.

"Pardon?"

Dawn was tempted to flick her tongue against his nipple. It looked so delectable and ready. But she knew how sensitive Michael was. If they were going to get anything accomplished today, tomorrow or the next day, one of them had to maintain some decorum.

"You weren't there," he said, "when I opened my eyes this morning. I had this horrible feeling you'd sneaked back to Costa Rica."

Dawn gazed at him in surprise. "I would never do that. I wanted to wake you, but you were sleeping so soundly."

Reassured, he smiled. "I guess I needed the rest. Did you enjoy making love last night?"

"Oh, Michael, I've never known anything like it in my life."

"I haven't, either."

Dawn was amazed at how much she needed to believe him. "You're not just saying that?"

Michael shook his head. "I don't believe in using lines on a woman. You're more than just a lover, Dawn. You're every woman I've ever dreamed of—beautifully gathered into one person."

"Thank you."

It was a lovely compliment. She should have been swooning. But Dawn barely managed a smile before looking away. What about love? she longed to ask. What about commitment and fidelity and till death do us part?

A shiver of panic ran up her spine. Dawn hadn't asked a lover those questions in years. When she had, the answers hadn't particularly mattered. This time, however, they did. This time accolades for sexual prowess weren't enough. She needed something more. Trouble was, Dawn didn't know exactly what that something was.

WINNIPEG WAS A BEAUTIFUL CITY, pulsing with an energy both vibrant and northern. Dawn, a halfhearted city person at best, was delighted by everything Michael showed her.

Over the next few days the weather warmed dramatically, melting the snow and launching spring as though for their personal enjoyment. Michael and Dawn went everywhere together, from the bustling downtown core to the trendy boutiques of Osborne Village. They attended a jazz festival at Memorial Park and had dinner in a romantic revolving restaurant. Amid the whirlwind of activity, they reveled in the simpler things. Kissing in elevators and giggling over cappuccinos, the two of them were totally involved and absorbed in each other.

But while they might have been oblivious, the world, apparently, was noticing. Michael mentioned it one evening as they lay in front of the fireplace, sipping wine. "Have you ever seen the reactions we get from people when we're out?"

Dawn was toying with the buttons on his shirt. They'd gone to a wonderful place called Basil's for lunch, come home and made love all afternoon, but she wasn't above doing it again. "Not especially. How are they reacting?"

"They're smiling, turning their heads to stare. It's weird."

"What's so weird about people smiling? They're just being friendly."

"This is Canada, Dawn."

"So?"

"We're not like Latin Americans. We're reserved." He paused to stroke her cheek. "I saw the looks you used to get from men in Costa Rica, but this is different."

Dawn sat up, cross-legged. "Now that you mention it, there was an old couple this afternoon in the restaurant who couldn't take their eyes off us. I didn't think much about it then, but they really seemed fascinated."

"Exactly, and it's been happening all week. What do you suppose they're seeing—apart from a gorgeous woman and a lucky guy?"

She gazed into the fire, allowing time for the proper response. Then she turned to find the firelight reflected in her lover's eyes. "My guess is, they're seeing happiness."

On Wednesday morning Michael presented a half-day seminar on loss control. Dawn opted to stay home and prepare a picnic lunch for later in Assiniboine Park. It was a gorgeous spring day, and she was looking forward to warmth and the feel of grass beneath her feet.

This was the first time since Dawn's arrival that she and Michael had been apart for more than a few minutes. Being a loner, it should have been a relief. Instead, while mixing crab dip and chopping vegetables, Dawn discovered that she missed him. Desperately.

This wasn't like her. Neither was it normal for Dawn to share so much of herself with anyone—let alone a man. This week, however, Dawn had shared everything with Michael. Every thought that flew into her head, every emotion and opinion, no matter how silly or far-fetched.

Not once did she worry about what he would think. Michael never criticized or belittled anything she said. Sometimes he laughed, but it was a sound of delight, an acknowledgment of her ability to entertain. And when they talked about contentious issues, more often than not, he agreed with Dawn. And that was amazing.

There were also subtler things that Dawn had learned to appreciate. The sensation of waking up beside Michael, sharing a pot of coffee, planning the day together. They had adapted to each other's routines with surprising ease. Dawn kept waiting for Michael to reveal his true habits, compulsive obsessive or whatever, but she had yet to see one. He really was an easygoing man.

Then, of course, there was their love, the physical expression of feelings that grew stronger every day. Their first night of lovemaking was no aberration. Michael was always spectacular in bed, but he was also caring and attentive.

Their lovemaking, it seemed, was continuous—a daily pattern of behavior, not something merely to be performed after dark. The way Michael touched, the gentle way he spoke, kept Dawn in a constant state of desire. Whether they were in a grocery store or the bedroom, it didn't matter. She always felt ready to love Michael and to be loved.

This perpetual state of arousal, however, would soon be a burden. In a few days this week would be over, relegated to the past along with Dawn's former lovers and assorted hurts. She would return to Montecristo, and no matter how deeply she ached or how often she reached out, Michael wouldn't be there.

The prospect of leaving was terrifying. And suddenly the happiness that remained was equally frightening.

Dawn couldn't face either extreme. Battling her emotions, she tossed a handful of celery stalks into the sink and rushed out of the kitchen. Then she threw herself on Michael's bed and cried.

DAWN BARELY MANAGED to pull herself together in time for the picnic. She and Michael were stretched out near the river beneath the budding cottonwoods. Michael was enjoying his crusty sandwich, but Dawn couldn't eat a thing.

"You should have seen the looks on their faces," he was saying. "There I was telling these corporate VP's that *they* were responsible for losing eleven million dollars a year—not the shift foremen, not the guys on the line."

Despite her best efforts, Dawn's chin had started to quiver. "How did they react?" she asked, determined to keep her mind on the topic at hand.

"I scared the hell out of them. You see, most corporations think they don't need loss control until they're shown otherwise. And did I show them, honey. It may take a while for my message to sink in, but it will."

Dawn sniffled and cleared her throat. "That's wonderful, Michael. I'm proud of you."

"Thanks."

Still high on his success, Michael was oblivious to Dawn's mood. She was just as glad he was. She'd hate to have him believe she was a wimpy female.

After a minute or two, she managed to think up a reasonable question. "Why are corporations so threatened by loss control?"

Michael picked up a carrot stick and used it to emphasize his point. "The main reason is that with loss control everyone is accountable. The traditional corporate structure is set up so that there's always someone to . . ." His voice trailed off, and he frowned. "What's the matter, sweetie?"

"N-nothing."

"You're crying."

"No, I'm not. I'm uh . . ." She wiped her eyes and blew her nose. "Well, maybe I am . . . a little. But go ahead. Keep talking."

"For goodness sake, I'm not going to keep talking. Come here, honey."

Dawn didn't try to be brave anymore. She allowed Michael to gather her in his arms. Slowly, deliciously, he kissed away her tears. Then he dried her eyes with the palm of his hand. "Now, tell me what's bothering you."

"Nothing, except that . . . it's Wednesday."

Despite his obvious concern, he chuckled. "You have a problem with Wednesdays?"

"When it's followed three days later by this Saturday, yes."

"That's the day you're leaving."

"Yes."

Michael looked away, his expression unreadable. "I've been thinking about that myself."

"Have you?"

"More than you know."

Dawn pulled herself from his embrace and scooted backward on the blanket. She needed to put some distance between them. Otherwise, it would be impossible to remain composed.

Michael didn't question the maneuver. Maybe he needed distance, too. He picked up the bottle of papaya-flavored mineral water and refilled their glasses.

In spite of her misery Dawn smiled, recalling the day he had bought the drink. They were in a variety store when Michael noticed a new drink on the shelves. He wasn't crazy about papaya, he admitted. But he bought the beverage because the label depicted a couple in a tropical waterfall.

"Looks just like you and me," he'd said with a devilish grin.

Michael was so sentimental. And he was such a sucker for packaging. It was one of a thousand things Dawn had learned about him this week—and one of a thousand she would miss.

"I didn't think leaving would hit me this hard," she confessed, wiping a tear from her cheek. "I was fine until this morning."

"When you were alone?"

"Yes, I started thinking about returning to Costa Rica. I hadn't thought about that all week."

"Are you looking forward to going home?"

"No, and that scares me."

Michael studied her for a while. "Maybe this is a good time to talk about our feelings."

"Isn't that what we've been doing all week?"

"Not as honestly as we could. We've done a lot of getting acquainted, a lot of loving, but we've never really admitted our deep down feelings."

"No, I suppose we haven't."

"Do you want to go first?" Michael asked.

She felt a quiver of panic. "Not really."

Michael laughed softly. "That's okay. I'll go first." He took her hands in his, turned them palm up and kissed each one in turn. "Truth is, I love you, Dawn. I've been in love with you since Costa Rica, and it's been growing stronger ever since."

Dawn wasn't prepared for her own reaction. She felt as though the wind had been knocked out of her. And all he'd said was that he loved her!

She opened her mouth to speak, but nothing came out.

"Are you okay?" he asked.

Dawn laughed. "Yes, I'm okay. I'm more than okay. I never thought hearing you say that would make such a difference. Then again, maybe I did, and that's why I didn't want to hear it. Oh, Michael, I'm babbling again! Have you ever noticed how I do that?"

He shared her laughter. "Yes, I've noticed."

She climbed onto her knees and hugged him. "I love you, too, Michael. I really do. I'm not sure exactly when it happened, but probably within fifteen minutes of meeting you."

"No, actually, it happened in the first five minutes. I was watching."

She swatted him playfully on the chest. "You would."

Sharing kisses and laughter, the two of them fell back and rolled across the blanket. It was as though new-spoken love had charged their passion. Michael's mouth moved over Dawn in a dizzying carousel of release. He captured her to himself as though he would never let go. At that moment Dawn would have been happy if he never did.

11

THEIR LAST FEW DAYS together should have been beautiful. Dawn should have taken advantage of every opportunity to make Michael happy, show him how much she cared, how grateful she was. But by the time Saturday morning arrived, the atmosphere, thanks to her, was chilly.

Dawn realized, while packing her bags, that she had felt the same way in Costa Rica when Michael left. Threatened, helpless, terrified. She had honestly believed that once their love was openly acknowledged things would be easier. Things were worse—at least for her. Maybe she was just no good at goodbyes.

"So you're just going to leave it at that?" Michael snapped. He was lying on the bed, fully dressed, his head propped on pillows. "We're not even going to discuss the matter anymore?"

Dawn stalked from the closet to the suitcase, emptying one, filling another. Every item of clothing jolted her with the memory of some special occasion—probably because most of the week had been special. "We've been discussing it for three days. There's nothing more to say."

"Except that we love each other."

She glanced at him briefly. "We've gone over that, too."

Turning her back on Michael, Dawn removed a blouse from the closet. A stunning green silk, he had bought it for her the day before. Feeling guilty, Dawn tried to tell him she'd have no place to wear it in Montecristo. That wasn't exactly true. It would be perfect for her occasional jaunts into San José. But she felt awful accepting anything more from a man to whom she could give nothing.

"But, Dawn," he said, "when two people are in love, they don't just write it off as a pleasant experience and go their separate ways. They try to work things out. They live together, get married."

Married. A word she'd once idealized, then reviled and finally put out of her head. Since when had she come full circle?

Dawn clutched the blouse to her breast. "In an ideal situation people do those things. But like I've said a thousand times before, our situation isn't ideal."

"We can agree to stay open with each other. Is that too much to ask?"

"Open to what? We have no openings."

"There might be, if we just try to compromise."

Dawn kicked her shoes out from under the bed. "Don't talk to me about compromise. As far as I'm concerned, it's just another word for selling out."

She was sick to death of this argument. And she was sick to death of the position Michael was putting her in. The more he insisted on commitment, the less Dawn was able to accommodate the notion. He might believe they could meet halfway, but in the end it would be Dawn who gave up everything. Between men and women that was always the way it was. And men called it compromise.

"So you're just going to fly back to Costa Rica and pretend I never existed?"

The hurt in his voice was like a dagger in her heart. But feeling cornered hurt Dawn just as deeply. "Damn it,

Michael, is that what you think? That I can just forget you?"

"That's the impression you've been giving."

"Well, you're wrong. Dead wrong! I'm never going to forget you. I probably won't stop loving you, either. But if I had my choice, I *would* forget because it's a heck of a lot easier than the prospect of living without you!"

"When did they start handing out medals for martyrdom?"

"I beg your pardon?"

"We don't *have* to live without each other. Can't you hear what I'm saying?"

Dawn threw up her hands. "Yes, I hear what you're saying, and in theory it sounds lovely. But what are we going to do—draw a line from Winnipeg to Montecristo on an atlas and live halfway in between?"

"There's no need for sarcasm."

Although Michael had contributed his fair share of sarcasm, he was right. So Dawn took a deep breath and tried to control herself. "Listen, you can't very well transfer your loss control business to the Costa Rican jungle."

"I would if I could."

"That's lip service, Mr. Garrett," she said, having the strange sensation she had used those words the night they'd met. She also recalled eating them later.

"It's not lip service, Dawn. I mean it."

"You mean it," she repeated slowly. "That's wonderful. Now how about we consider my side of the story? I would dearly love to wake up every morning beside you and do all the things we enjoy doing. The problem is, Manitoba doesn't have rain forests, which happen to be my specialty. I could promise that if your country ever manages to grow one, I'll be the first to apply. But that's as good as no promise at all, isn't it?"

She'd hurt him. She knew that. And Dawn wished there was some way to take the hurt away. But how much could she do in the two remaining hours?

"I guess you're right," he said. "It's as good as no promise at all."

"So can we just drop the subject?"

He shrugged, the epitome of male nonchalance. "I'll still be coming to Costa Rica in a month. Do you want me to get in touch with you or not?"

Please, Michael, get in touch with me. Never stop touching me!

"Not if we're going to argue," she said. "We've wasted the past three days arguing, and I can't take it anymore."

Michael's eyes gentled. He got up from the bed and wrapped his arms around Dawn. "Neither can I, baby. I hate fighting with you."

She clung to him for a while, then stepped back and zipped her suitcase shut. "So, it's settled then. I'll see you in a month, and we'll, uh . . . have a great time, right?"

Michael hoisted the bag off the bed. "Right, Dawn, whatever you say."

IT REALLY WAS for the best. Dawn kept repeating the words to herself until they were branded into her heart. On the plane from Winnipeg to Miami, on the connecting flight to San José, she relived their arguments, their strained parting words, and always came to the same conclusion. She and Michael weren't meant to be. Period.

In fifty years or so she might forget how deeply in love they used to be. With any luck, even the vivid sexual details might fade. People eventually reached an age when passion didn't matter, when sexuality became a hall-mark of the young and impetuous.

Meanwhile, Dawn had work to consume her. And if she labored really hard, she could reach that passionless age in no time. But what a depressing thought!

From the airport in Costa Rica Dawn took a shuttle to downtown San José, then waited in the depot for the bus to Puntarenas. It was a two-hour wait, and the wait was misery. Her sinuses were aching from the dry airplane cabin, and the wine she'd had with dinner wasn't set-tling well.

She considered waiting until morning to catch the ex-press bus to Montecristo, but that would mean spend-ing the night in San José, and Dawn had had enough of cities for a while. Staying in Puntarenas was more of a treat, and today, of all days, a treat was in order.

To be perfectly honest, a part of her was delighted to be back in Costa Rica. After five years it was home. But whether she could ever emulate the happiness of the past week, Dawn didn't know. And she was much too ex-hausted to dwell on the topic. All she wanted now—apart from Michael—was to curl up in her own bed and sleep forever. Meanwhile, Dawn curled up in the cracked vinyl seat and shut her eyes to the world around her.

The mosquitoes were dreadful after dark. Dawn swatted her arms and face and neck until she thought she'd go mad. She should have remembered to buy re-pellent while she was in town that afternoon. Damn the old memory, anyway. They always said it was the first to go.

She moved the kerosene lamp closer and pressed gnarled fingers to her eyes. Her eyes were stinging more than usual tonight, and the letters on the page were swimming. Maybe her glasses needed changing. Memory, eyesight—it was always something.

The reports were drudgery, as always, but accurate records were essential if the rain forest was to be monitored properly. And if Dawn didn't monitor properly, who would?

People had been coming and going from Montecristo for fifty years. She was the only one who'd been here since the beginning, the only one who really knew the place. She'd probably die here. And why not? There was nowhere else to die.

In the village they called her the madwoman of Montecristo. But Dawn knew she wasn't crazy. Just weary, lonely and old.

And not that she was complaining. Her life had been fulfilling enough. It might even make a great story someday, if anyone cared enough to write it.

But nobody cared.

Dawn set her pencil aside.

Someone did care once, long ago. His name was Michael. Michael Garrett. She remembered exactly how he looked. He was tall, strong, handsome, and they had loved each other so much.

Michael wanted to take her away from Montecristo, but Dawn turned him down, told him she loved her rain forest too much. He never let up on her. Finally, tiring of the constant pressure, she refused to see him anymore.

Dawn used to think he would never stop loving her. That one day when she least expected it, Michael would show up on her doorstep and try once more to win her over. If he had, she probably would have accepted his offer.

But once more never came. Fifty years passed, and Dawn never saw or heard from Michael again. In the *foolish days of her youth she used to believe the memories would fade, that someday she would forget the details of their passion.*

She was wrong. The passion they'd shared was clearer than ever now, and twice as painful. She never should have—

Dawn felt someone nudging her shoulder and tried to ignore him. Couldn't he see she was busy? If this blasted report to the World Wildlife Fund wasn't finished on time—

"*¡Despiértese, señorita! Estamos en Puntarenas.*"

Puntarenas? Dawn bolted upright, heart pounding, palms sweaty. "Where . . . what am I . . . ?"

She looked around blearily. There were no other passengers on the bus, only the driver staring at her as though she was ill.

The first thing she did was touch her face. The skin felt taut and smooth, hardly the complexion of an eighty-five-year-old. Then she pulled out the ticket stub wedged into the seat pocket in front of her. It bore today's date, the same day she left Winnipeg—and Michael.

What had she said to him at the end? In her groggy state Dawn struggled to remember. Did she leave Michael with any hope? Or had she walked away with her pride—and precious little else? The answer that came was chilling. She hadn't given Michael much of anything. No commitments, no promises, only the feeble assurance of a good time. If that nightmare was any indication, her assurance was hardly worth the effort. Dawn would be lucky if she ever heard from Michael again.

The driver was getting impatient for her to leave. Dawn mumbled an apology and collected her luggage.

The Hotel Tioga was fifteen minutes away. It felt like the longest, loneliest walk of Dawn's life.

As soon as she entered the lobby, she realized her tactical error. Dawn never should have booked a room in the same hotel where Michael stayed. Everything reminded her of him—the water reflecting off the pool, the winding staircase. By some cruel twist of fate she was even assigned to his old room—338.

She unlocked the door and stepped inside, imagining how Michael might have settled in, where he would have unpacked. After only a week she felt as though she knew his habits intimately.

What would have happened, Dawn wondered, if she'd accepted the invitation to this room the night they'd met? If she'd managed to sneak past the night clerk, would she and Michael have ended up making love?

Maybe. Dawn flung her bags into the closet. But it was a moot point. They had ended up lovers one week later, anyway, so what difference would it have made? In retrospect it all seemed inevitable.

Dawn couldn't stay in the room. She felt as though the walls were closing in on her. Having slept on the bus, she knew it was pointless to go to bed. And there was always the danger of that ghastly nightmare coming back.

She took a quick shower, noting wryly that the hot water was finally working. Michael would have been pleased. Then she left the hotel and headed down the street to Lito's.

If her friend hadn't been working behind the bar, she wouldn't have bothered going in. But Lito was there— burly, friendly, tattooed. He hadn't noticed Dawn. She was still lingering in the shadows a few feet away, trying to summon up her old panache.

But how could she walk in the way she used to? Nothing was the same anymore. Or to be more accurate, everything was the same except Dawn. Michael's table was in the same place and, farther on, was the bar stool where she had ordered Campari and soda like some half-convincing sophisticate. The same waiters were there, the same stained menus— *"¡Chica!"*

Startled, she battled an urge to dive into the nearest shrub. But it was too late. One of the waiters had spotted her.

Dawn realized then that she could either face this bar—and the world—like the free-spirited, independent woman she believed herself to be, or she could wimp out and scuttle back to the hotel. She'd have rather scuttled.

But the hotel was no solution. Michael's ghosts were just as prevalent there. She might as well go into the bar and pretend to be happy again.

Here goes, Dawn told herself. The performance of a lifetime. She pinned a smile to her face, greeted the waiter and entered the bar with supreme confidence. *"Hola, Lito. ¿Cómo está?"*

DUBROVNIK'S WAS ONE of Winnipeg's most elegant restaurants. Michael's date was one of Winnipeg's most elegant women. She had gorgeous red hair, a terrific figure and tons of money. He wished he were at home eating hot dogs.

"It's so sweet of you to come out with me on such short notice," Jacquie cooed. But then she always cooed. "Of course, I'd been trying to phone you all week, and you were never home."

Michael bit his cheek to stay serious. He and Dawn had actually been home quite a bit, but they'd made a point of unplugging the phone whenever they were. "I had company and took the week off. I was in and out a lot." *Watch it, Garrett. Poor choice of words.*

"Last time we talked you never mentioned company."

"Didn't I?"

"No. So who was this mystery guest?"

"A woman."

Michael noticed Jacquie's impeccable nails digging into the table, but she managed to keep her expression noncommittal. "Oh? Anyone I know?"

"I doubt it. She's from Costa Rica. Well, actually, she's American, but she seems like...never mind, Jacquie. You don't know her."

"Maybe not, but I do know you. We've been friends for, what . . . six years?"

"Something like that."

Michael had met Jacquie years ago when he dated her best girlfriend. The girlfriend had long since gone her own way, but Jacquie was still trying to pick up the slack. He had no delusions about the woman's intentions, but neither had he ever taken her up on them. She wasn't his type—never would be. But somehow they'd fallen into a unique friendship that usually meant an expensive dinner and one less nightcap than Jacquie would have liked.

"I'm hearing alarms ringing, Michael, and I worry when I hear alarms. Are you really hung up on this woman or what?"

Michael sloshed the ice cubes in his Rusty Nail. "No, yeah . . . I don't know."

Her laugh tinkled. "Now there's a typically decisive male remark. What does she look like?"

"She's beautiful. She has . . ." He was about to list Dawn's attributes—legs, eyes, hair, the usual statistics.

But for some reason Michael couldn't bring himself to say anything.

Maybe he shouldn't have gone out this soon. After all, Dawn had just left that morning, and he was still feeling like his soul had been ripped out. But Jacquie had opened her tenth lingerie boutique or her twentieth—he couldn't remember—and she wanted to celebrate.

So why the hell did she have to celebrate with him? He'd done some loss control work for her, but she had a million friends in the fashion business who would have been better company.

It occurred to Michael, irrelevantly perhaps, that the woman sitting across from him wouldn't like Dawn no matter what he said. Dawn was honest, down-to-earth and true to herself. Jacquie, lacking those attributes herself, could never have appreciated them. And he was suddenly resenting her infernal curiosity.

"Well?" Jacquie said, a trifle shrill. "What's so terrific about this Puerto Rican?"

"Costa Rican," he corrected, yanking the napkin off his lap. "You wouldn't understand, but she is terrific. Listen, Jacquie, at the risk of our friendship, could we take a rain check on this dinner? I just remembered an important engagement."

"But we just got here!"

"I know, but—"

"And it was your turn to buy dinner."

"I realize that, and I'm awfully sorry. But I will make it up to you. Promise."

"When?"

"I don't know."

Jacquie wasn't impressed. She snatched up her mink, tossed a few pithy epithets about men and stalked out the door. Her Jaguar had roared out of the parking lot before Michael could embellish his excuse.

"CHICA, WHAT A SURPRISE!" Lito shook her hand, kissed both cheeks and pounded her on the back, as always.

Everyone needed a friend like Lito, Dawn surmised, just to keep the world in perspective. He was an expert at pulling people out of the doldrums. She settled onto a bar stool, greeted the other waiters and ordered her regular—club soda and lime.

"How's Marisa?" she asked.

"Just fine."

"And the baby?"

"Ah, Alejandro! Only three weeks old, but he's a genius." Lito grinned and reached beneath the bar. "I have photos."

He did, too. Hundreds of them, it seemed. Alejandro was a beautiful baby, although Dawn couldn't really distinguish him from any other baby. But the topic, at least, was distracting. It pleased her to hear that Enrique had settled down and was proud of his new role as papa. Marisa was taking a correspondence course in dress design, a gift from her father.

"That's thoughtful of you, Lito. I'm sure she'll love the course."

"I think so. She's a good girl, my Marisa. If only her mother were alive to see her." Lito excused himself to serve another customer, but he soon returned. "So tell me, how are you coping? I have been trying to get in touch with you. I was worried."

Lito was always worried about Dawn's welfare, so it came as no surprise. "I'm fine. I just got back from a week in Canada."

"Canada? What were you doing there?"

Complicating my life, she felt like saying. Deluding myself. There were any number of ways to paraphrase falling in love.

"I was visiting a friend. I think you met him. Remember the gringo, the Canadian, who bought me a drink a few weeks ago?"

Lito knotted his brows. "Oh, sure, I remember now. He's the one who helped you bring Enrique home."

"That's him."

"Well, how about that? So it turned out to be more than a drink, no?"

"I guess you could say that."

"Is he a good person? Does he have a steady job?"

"Yes and yes." In spite of her lousy mood, Dawn laughed. If only goodness and a steady job were enough.

"Wonderful, *chica*. When can we expect to hear wedding bells?"

Dawn nearly choked on her drink. "No bells. We're just friends."

"Come now, you know better than to fool me. Your face is lit up like a beacon. You love him, no?"

"I suppose . . . no, that's not true. I *do* love him."

"What is his name?"

"Michael Garrett."

"Michael. I like that. Now tell me. If you and Michael love each other, why do you not get married, make a life together? You've been alone too long, *chica*."

Some people wore their conscience on their shoulder. Hers, Dawn suspected, worked behind a Costa Rican bar. "I wish we could have a life together, but it's not that simple."

"What is not so simple?"

"My life is with Montecristo," she said. "I'm a biologist. I can't just stop doing what I care about most."

The bartender stared at her for a moment, then picked up a glass and began to polish vigorously. "You have not heard the news, have you?"

"What news?"

"About Montecristo."

Panic unfurled in her stomach. "No, I haven't heard anything. What happened?"

"Hold on. I think I still have it." Lito bent down and rummaged through clutter beneath the bar. He emerged a minute later with a newspaper and handed it to her.

It was yesterday's edition of a San José paper. Dawn stared, aghast, at the headlines: Rain Forest Director Gives Up Hostage, Turns Himself In. Montecristo Closed Indefinitely.

12

THERE WAS NO POINT in letting the phone ring any longer. No one was there. For hours Michael had been trying to contact the administration office in Montecristo, but it was Saturday night. Why should anyone be there, let alone Dawn?

He felt terrible about ditching poor Jacquie at Dubrovnik's. He'd never done anything so thoughtless in his life and would have to find a way to make it up to her. But a blinding rush of panic had hit him just then. A realization that Dawn was gone and that maybe she hadn't understood how deeply he loved her.

Then again, she had to know. Michael had told her a thousand times during the past few days. His mistake was making demands on Dawn too soon. And it wasn't even like him. They'd had a lot of talks about commitment, and both of them agreed it was a difficult word. He was the one who changed the rules midgame, not Dawn.

What if he told her he needed her? Maybe then she'd understand. Good grief, Michael thought with a shudder. That ought to be enough to scare her away forever. Until recently he'd scarcely understood the word himself. A man might need a backrub, or a drink—or sex. But once they were obtained, the craving was alleviated, however temporarily.

Michael already knew it wouldn't work that way with Dawn. The more time he spent with that woman, the more he needed her. And the longer they were apart, the same still held true. What was a guy supposed to do?

Knowing he wasn't going to reach Dawn tonight, Michael finally went to bed. But sleep wasn't easy. Time and again he reached for the empty space that used to be Dawn. His hand hit nothing but cold sheets, awakening him to a loneliness so profound that it was almost physical.

When morning arrived, dismal and overcast, Michael gave up and stumbled out of bed. He filled the coffee maker with ten cups of water, deciding that a caffeine blitz was the only thing that would get him through the day.

Michael carried the urn and a huge mug into the living room where last week's newspapers were piled in a corner. They had to be the ultimate proof of Dawn's effect on him. Michael never missed a day of the *Globe and Mail.* For him, reading the paper was as involuntary as breathing, yet while Dawn was here he hadn't given it a thought.

He opened yesterday's copy first, intending to peruse it more closely than the older editions. He began, as always, with the headlines. Then he moved on to the business section. Finally he returned to the beginning and concentrated only on the articles that interested him.

Unfortunately nothing captured his interest. His mind wandered through the stock market listings, and he yawned at the headlines. It seemed like there was nothing new in the world, and nothing to compete with Dawn for Michael's attention.

He was skimming the International News in Brief column when he caught sight of Costa Rica. The article was brief, the details sketchy, but it was enough to send chills down his spine.

Montecristo, Costa Rica's second largest rain forest, will be closed indefinitely following a six-hour hostage-taking early Friday evening. The incident ended peacefully after Montecristo's director, Flavius Van der Pol, released a female staff member and turned himself in to authorities. The reserve has been plagued with financial and administrative problems since its inception five years ago. The chairman of the board, Dr. Emilio Bustamante, is quoted as saying that unless drastic measures are taken quickly to protect the reserve, ten thousand hectares of rain forest could be lost forever.

For a long while Michael just sat there with the paper in his lap. The incident had taken place on Friday while Dawn was still here. But for the grace of God, that hostage could have been Dawn. And Flavius could just as easily have killed her.

Anger followed his relief. He never should have allowed Dawn to stay there with that man. He'd tried to warn her, but she was too stubborn to listen.

Guilt was the last emotion to set in. How could Michael be grateful for Dawn's safety while another woman suffered? It must have been a terrible ordeal. Thank God the woman wasn't hurt.

Michael picked up the paper again and checked the dates. It didn't say exactly when Montecristo was closing, but the decision looked pretty final. Damn! He *should* have read the paper. If Dawn had known what happened, maybe she wouldn't have gone back. She'd have been devastated, but at least Michael would have been there to console her.

He was more worried than ever about Dawn. She must have heard the news by now. Then again, if she didn't read a paper or talk to anyone, she might not find out until she arrived in Montecristo. That would have been this morning sometime. What a shock it would be to find the gates locked, the place deserted.

Still, if she did go to Montecristo, there was a possibility that Michael might catch her in the office, cleaning out her desk or whatever. He leaped out of his chair and dashed to the phone. Unless she contacted him, this might be his last chance to find Dawn. And his last chance for happiness.

A TAXI FROM THE VILLAGE dropped Dawn off at the entrance to the rain forest. She was going to ask him to wait, in case she had no way of returning. But the Land Rover was parked near the gates, so someone was obviously here. She was certain it wouldn't be Flavius.

Dawn paid the driver and stepped out. That was when she saw Jorge lumbering down the dirt driveway. She didn't try to hide her anxiety. She ran to the security guard and threw her arms around his neck.

"Jorge, I'm so glad to see you," she said. "I was afraid no one would be here."

"Your timing was lucky. I only came to disconnect the utilities and check that everything is safe."

"Is everyone gone then?"

"Yes, Montecristo is officially closed."

"Where is your family?"

"In the village for now. We moved most of our belongings yesterday."

Dawn couldn't think of anything to say. She felt helpless and bereft, as though she'd arrived too late to visit a dying relative.

"Did you have a good trip to Canada?" Jorge asked.

"The trip was fine, but we'll talk about that some other time. How are you, Jorge? Were you harmed at all during the . . ." The news was too fresh in her mind, too horrifying. She couldn't bring herself to finish the sentence.

"I was unharmed, thank God."

Dawn took a minute to study him. Jorge looked tired and strained, but that was understandable. "I never should have left you alone with Flavius," she said, "knowing how sick he was."

"There was nothing you could have done, *chica*. It was nobody's fault."

Dawn had stayed up half the night trying to convince herself of the same thing. But her conscience wouldn't let her off that easily. She could have been more insistent with Dr. Bustamante. She should have taken action as soon as she recognized Flavius's problem—just as Michael had warned her to do.

Michael. She spent the other half of the night thinking about him—missing him and wishing he was there. Dawn even considered phoning to tell him about Montecristo, but he might have insisted she take the next flight to Canada. Dawn was nowhere near ready to face that possibility. She had a thousand questions about Montecristo that needed to be answered first.

"Would it bother you too much to tell me what happened?" she asked Jorge.

"Not at all. Come with me to the office. I have a thermos of coffee and we can talk."

Somehow she'd expected the office to look different. The furniture should have been overturned or the windows smashed—something to suggest the hideous action that had taken place. But everything looked the same. Lonely, neglected, but the same.

"It was three o'clock on Friday when I heard shots fired from the office," Jorge began after pouring Dawn a tepid cup of coffee.

She had gotten some of the details from the paper. But she wanted to hear the unabridged version from Jorge. "What was he shooting at?"

"Nothing. He just fired shots through the window." He pointed to one near the front door. "Fortunately the window was open."

"Was Alicia already in here with him?" she asked, referring to the receptionist.

"Yes, she was in the back room getting files. When she ran to see what the noise was about, Flavius turned and pointed the gun at her. He dragged her to the window and shouted that unless his demands were met, he was going to kill Alicia and burn down the complex."

Dawn looked out at the vast expanse of wilderness outside. "The man really was sick. There's nobody out here to shout to."

"Perhaps he thought the world could hear him. Who knows? None of the volunteer staff had come in all week, and my wife and children were in the house. So I was the only one who could hear him."

Tremors of vicarious fear raced through her. "What did you do?"

"I came out of the booth with my pistol drawn. But as I came closer to the office, I saw that Flavius was holding a gun to Alicia's temple. He ordered me to drop the weapon. For the young woman's sake, I knew I had no choice."

"My God, you are so brave, Jorge."

The man shrugged. "One does not concern oneself with bravery at such times. To be honest, my greatest fear was the safety of my family. I had no way of warning them to stay indoors."

"Did they?"

"Yes. My wife sensed that something was wrong and would not allow the children outside. She is very perceptive that way."

Dawn thought of someone else she considered perceptive, then quickly put him out of her mind. "What happened next?"

"Flavius wanted me to communicate a list of demands to the board in San José."

"He was in here with the phone. Why couldn't he do it himself?"

"You know how terrible his Spanish is. He wanted no misunderstandings."

"What were his demands?"

"A ransom of one million colones, safe passage to Belgium and a hearing with some famous scientist about his discoveries."

Dawn recalled the day Flavius told her about his work on natural selection. His fiancée had ruined him by leaking the discoveries too soon. Flavius had also said that Dawn reminded him of his fiancée. The recollection made her shudder.

"Did you contact the board?" she asked.

"I tried. Flavius ordered me into the office and told me to phone. I tried to reason with him, at first, but it was no use. The man has no grasp on reality. So I contacted Bustamante and told him what Flavius wanted."

Jorge's hands were gripping the coffee cup, but Dawn could still see them shaking. "It must have been terrible for you."

"It was. I had to speak very slowly so that Flavius would understand. Every time my Spanish was too fast, he would shove the gun deeper into Alicia's neck."

Her heart wrenched to think of the receptionist's plight. She was so young and impressionable. "Did you tell Bustamante what was happening?"

"Of course, but I was also told to warn him not to call the Civil Guard or all of us would be killed—Alicia, my wife . . . the ch-children."

Dawn placed an arm on his shoulder. "If it's too hard to talk about—"

"No, I am fine. It feels better to talk. Bustamante had many questions, but Flavius would not allow me to answer them. Finally Flavius got impatient, took the phone and did the talking himself. He gave Dr. Bustamante three hours to phone back and meet his demands and also warned him again not to contact the police."

"Three hours, good heavens. I can't imagine how you got through it."

"Alicia and I had divine protection. I am sure of that."

Moved by Jorge's faith, Dawn smiled. She wished she had a tenth as much. "The papers say you eventually persuaded him to surrender."

"Yes."

"How?"

"I kept him talking for two hours. I asked about his family, his childhood, the work he does. I don't know, *chica*, where the words were coming from, but I trusted them. The more we talked, the calmer Flavius became. Finally he broke down and started crying. That's when I knew he would give me the gun."

"He actually gave it to you?"

"Yes. He pleaded with me to shoot him, but I told him it would not be a kind thing to do in front of Alicia."

"That's amazing. I could never have handled the situation so smoothly. Did Doctor Bustamante ever phone back?"

"No, he never did." At the mention of the chairman, Jorge's jaw began to pulse with anger. "But shortly after I took the gun a dozen Civil Guards arrived, fully armed, and surrounded the office. That was what Bustamante did, despite Flavius's warning. If he'd still had the gun, we'd all be dead."

"But what else could Doctor Bustamante have done? He had no reason to trust Flavius."

"He also had no choice. He could have pretended to pay the ransom. He could have . . . ah, never mind. It is over now." Rubbing his eyes, the man slumped heavily into the chair.

"What have they done with Flavius?"

"He is in a psychiatric hospital in San José and will soon be returned to Belgium."

Dawn looped an arm around her friend's shoulders. "You really were a hero, Jorge. Do you know that?"

"What difference does it make to be a hero? Our forest is closed and will probably be sold. All the work we have done will be for nothing."

"You don't actually think they'd sell Montecristo?" she said, horrified. "From what I read, it was just a temporary closure."

"It is not for me to say, but I have trouble believing in anything these days except misfortune."

It was frightening to see Jorge give up hope. Except for Dawn, he was the only one who'd worked in Montecristo since the beginning, and she'd come to depend on his optimism. "I won't let them sell Montecristo."

"That will be the board's decision. How can you prevent it?"

"I don't know, but I'll think of something." For a minute or two she pondered her claim, wondering where she got the audacity. Acquiring land for Montecristo was easy enough. Thinking she could reverse Bustamante's decision bordered on egotistical. "What about you, Jorge? What are you going to do in the meantime?"

"Move to the city, I suppose. It won't be as safe for our children, but that is where the jobs are. How about you, *chica?* What will you do?"

Her first thought was of Michael. He loved her and wanted her. Anyone with sense would have told Dawn he was the ideal alternative. And ideally he was. She wouldn't have to wage battles over Montecristo anymore. She could move to Canada and have a wonderful, comfortable life with Michael. It wasn't as though she didn't love him.

Yesterday Dawn had boarded the plane feeling as though she was abandoning one love for another. The pain it evoked was almost unbearable. Today she was contemplating the reverse—abandoning Montecristo for Michael. And that prospect hurt just as much. It seemed unfair, but no matter which way she looked at it, Dawn would never have both loves.

"I don't know what I'm going to do, Jorge. I'm not sure if I'll ever know."

"EL NÚMERO NO ESTÁ en servicio, señor."

"I'm sorry," Michael said to the long-distance operator. "My Spanish isn't very good. Do you speak English?"

"A little. The number you want is not in service."

That was what he thought she'd said. He was just hoping he'd heard wrong. "Could you check if there are any other listings for Montecristo? A contact number in San José maybe?"

"I have already checked, sir. We have no other listings for Montecristo."

He thanked the operator and hung up, feeling as though a life cord had been severed. He had no way of contacting Dawn now. There was nothing to do but wait and hope that she would get in touch. But she might not, and that scared the hell out of him.

Michael used to be so sure of himself. Once he had captured a woman's interest, he never worried about whether he could maintain it. And why should he? Once the interest was gone—and it was usually on his part— Michael took it as a signal to move on. No big deal.

It wasn't working that way with Dawn. He'd never felt so much in doubt and kept rehashing the same old insecurities. Maybe he hadn't convinced her of his love. Maybe Dawn didn't appreciate how lucky they were to have each other. If he'd had a little more time to shower her with the good things in life, maybe he'd have had more impact.

Michael poured himself a drink and sat in his favorite chair. Whenever he needed profound wisdom, he sat in this chair, and it never failed him. All he had to do was process the problem and eventually a small voice would reply.

There were a number of ways he could approach this issue. First of all, he could wait. Dawn had only left yesterday. During the next few weeks she might come to her senses and realize what a great opportunity she had with him. That would be nice, but it was also risky, in case she didn't come to her senses. The more time passed, the easier it would be for Dawn to find another rain forest and be lost to him forever.

On the other hand, he could cancel his appointments and hop a plane to Costa Rica first thing in the morning. Even if Dawn wasn't living in Montecristo, he could still find her. It wasn't that big a country.

Once he located her he could try logic. Montecristo, the major impediment between them, was closed. There was no reason for her to stay in Costa Rica any longer.

Dawn might insist that there were other jobs in her field—and none of them were in Manitoba. That argument could be tricky, but Michael had a hunch that it was Montecristo in particular that held her captive. She had worked in some pretty exotic places over the years but never spoke of them with the same affection.

As for occupying herself if she moved here, Michael knew Dawn could come up with something. She could write her memoirs or submit articles to nature magazines. He'd happily set up a study for her to rival all studies.

And if that didn't do it, he would draw her a list of the other benefits she would enjoy by living with him. Financial independence, first-class travel, friends in high places. He could provide her with a life most women only dreamed about.

The only flaw in his reasoning was that Dawn didn't dream about those things. She held her own in Winnipeg's finest restaurants and genuinely appeared to enjoy them. But she was just as content in front of the fireplace munching pizza.

It seemed incredible, but Michael had the feeling that if he'd never taken her out while she was here, Dawn wouldn't have complained. It wouldn't have even occurred to her to complain.

What did a man do to impress a woman like that? How could he possibly win her over, let alone maintain her interest?

The small voice replied, but the answer was so simple, Michael thought he'd heard wrong. So he poured himself another drink and went through the whole process again. Half an hour later he got the same reply.

There was only one way to win Dawn, the voice said. There was only one way to maintain her interest.

Love her.

"Yes, but what if I never hear from her?" he demanded in the silent room. "What am I supposed to do then?"

The answer came again, more insistently this time.

Love her.

WHEN SOMETHING PRECIOUS DIED, it was the little things that hurt most. Dawn spent the next few days absorbing that truth as she packed to leave Montecristo. Her home and office were crammed with memories, every one reminding her how special the past five years had been. There were postcards and souvenirs from grateful tourists, copies of inspired letters she'd fired off to bureaucrats and businessmen, wildflowers pressed into books.

How long would it take, she wondered, to recreate this kind of bond elsewhere? Another five years? No, Dawn told herself, swiping at tears. It would take far longer next time.

She had never believed that age was a detriment, but Dawn was thirty-five, past the stage of naiveté and tireless optimism. She didn't have the energy or the interest to start over somewhere else.

One thing was certain. If Dawn had known five years ago what she knew now, Montecristo would be a different place. She would never have tolerated the inefficiency, apathy and outright mismanagement of the directors she worked with. She wouldn't have stood in the background, patiently spoon-feeding her superiors, always giving them the credit and shouldering the blame when they messed up.

Had she been more assertive, more confident of her abilities, Dawn wouldn't have been satisfied to remain second in command. She would have stood up to the board of directors and earned their respect instead of their derision.

She could have been director of Montecristo—Dawn knew that now—and the place would have flourished. She had learned her lesson well. But she'd learned it too late.

DAWN'S APARTMENT in San José was tiny, but with two rooms it was twice the size of her cabin in Montecristo. She also had running water and electricity, making it a veritable castle.

Unfortunately she couldn't afford a castle. Dawn had been living in the city for two weeks, working as a tutorial assistant at the university. The job was innocuous enough, but poorly paid. No matter how carefully Dawn budgeted, her daily expenses always exceeded her income.

The shock of leaving Montecristo was wearing off, but slowly. The first week had been the worst. The board of directors had wanted everyone off the reserve as soon as possible, so Dawn had had to pack up and leave before she'd had any idea where she was going. She'd shipped her belongings to the village and come to San José, knowing, like Jorge, that this was where the jobs were.

Luckily she'd found work within a few days, after contacting an old colleague at the university. They were delighted to have her on staff. There were already rumblings that if Dawn applied herself, she could obtain a full professorship within the year.

She ought to have been flattered, but the opportunity held little appeal for someone accustomed to freedom and fresh air. The lecture halls were airless, and the academic system stifling. At the end of every day her throat was sore and she wanted to scream.

At first she had hoped that the closing of Montecristo was a temporary measure until the memory of Flavius had faded and a new director could be found. If it wasn't a temporary measure, Dawn intended to offer an airtight presentation as to why they couldn't afford to abandon Montecristo.

But after meeting with the close-minded Dr. Bustamante, Dawn realized she was tilting at windmills. The chairman, despite his education, considered Dawn little more than an orchid collector, and Montecristo a hobby he had tired of. He wasn't interested in Dawn's plans for reopening the forest, wasn't interested in the forest at all.

There was nothing she could do. Bustamante had already called an emergency meeting, and the members had voted to dissolve the Montecristo board as soon as outstanding legalities were dealt with. As to the future of the rain forest, that was still up in the air. It could be sold, developed or taken over by the government. Only time would tell.

Dawn, Jorge and the other staff members were given a nominal severance pay and dismissed outright. The gates of Montecristo were locked, the buildings boarded. Just like that her dream was over.

The only dream that didn't end was Michael. Although he wasn't there physically, he went with Dawn everywhere. Instead of fading with each passing day, the image of him grew stronger—and so did her love.

Dawn wrote to Michael as soon as she was settled in San José. The letter had been difficult and didn't come close to expressing her real emotions. She thanked him again for her week in Canada and informed him of what had happened in Montecristo—which he probably would have caught on the news, anyway.

What she didn't tell him was the truth. That was strange from a woman to whom honesty was an obsession. What Dawn had finally concluded, after a week of anguish, was that Montecristo's closing might be a blessing in disguise. But she didn't tell Michael.

She should have admitted she'd made a big mistake the day she'd left Canada. He had asked her only to keep an open mind regarding their future, and Dawn had stubbornly refused. As long as she was obligated to the cause of Montecristo, she couldn't imagine herself abandoning it. No matter how much she loved Michael, her conscience would never have allowed her to leave the rain forest.

Suddenly the obligation was gone. Call it coincidence or call it fate, but Montecristo was no longer an issue. Dawn was free, literally free, to go to Michael and begin a new life.

So why didn't she? There were a number of technical reasons and intellectual reasons that Dawn could have presented. But they all boiled down to two elements as common as dirt. Fear and pride.

She was ashamed of the way she'd treated Michael after the way he loved her. She'd tried to show him physically how much she cared. But looking back, she realized fear had prevented her from reciprocating on a deeper level. What if Michael's love wasn't as solid as Dawn believed it to be? What if she left Montecristo, moved halfway around the world and things didn't work out? Where would she go, what would she do?

Then, when she learned that Montecristo was closed, pride became the new consideration. Dawn couldn't very well call Michael and tell him she'd changed her mind, now that she had no choices. He would feel like second best, a consolation prize, and in a way he'd be right. They would be beginning their relationship with loss and hurt feelings—hardly an auspicious start.

Michael deserved better. He deserved a woman with the courage to acknowledge her love and to act on it, sincerely and decisively. Dawn had had her chance a few weeks ago, and she'd blown it. What right did she have to expect another chance?

As it turned out, she did get another chance to prove herself. Like most twists of fate, it came from an entirely unexpected source. Dawn received a letter one day from Costa Rica's largest and most famous biological reserve. The director, Jim Stratton, was someone whose reputation she admired very much. An American like her, he had worked for thirty years in Costa Rica on reforestation.

He'd heard through the grapevine that Dawn was lecturing in San José and wondered if she would consider a position at his reserve. Dawn couldn't believe her good fortune. She had planned to contact Jim eventually and leave her application on file. But there were so many other things going on that she hadn't had the chance. And everyone knew Jim's staff was exceedingly loyal. For years they'd had virtually no turnover.

The interview, held in his San José office, went better than expected. Dr. Stratton had read several of her articles in scientific journals and was impressed with her knowledge of rain forests. His own reserve had tripled in size since its inception, and along with that, so had his work load. He was looking for an assistant director, someone who could pick up the slack while he went on the road and publicized their work.

The money was good, nearly twice what Dawn had earned at Montecristo. She liked Dr. Stratton at once. He was friendly, easygoing and extremely knowledgeable. Granted, she would once again be second in command, but she could learn a lot from the man. The opportunity seemed heaven-sent.

Yet when Jim officially offered her the position, Dawn demurred. He looked surprised, and he had reason. Any research scientist would have leaped at the chance to work with a man of his caliber. But Dawn couldn't bring herself to say yes.

"I'll need time to consider it, if that's all right with you," she said as politely as she could.

He lifted a bushy white brow. "I have a heavy work load, Dawn. I was hoping you could give me an answer right away."

"I understand. But you see, I have a few . . . personal items to clear up. They shouldn't take more than a day or two, and then I'll be able to commit myself one way or another."

Dr. Stratton looked as though he wanted to retract the offer, but something wouldn't let him. Dawn suspected it might be an indication of her professional merits. If so, that was a good sign.

"Okay, Dawn, if you can get back to me in twenty-four hours, the job's yours. Thanks for dropping by."

The first thing she did upon leaving Dr. Stratton's office was find a phone booth. She found one on a noisy street corner where diesel trucks changed gears, but it was better than nothing. She dropped a coin into the slot and dialed the operator, asking her to place a collect call to Winnipeg, Canada.

Michael answered right away. "Yes, of course I'll accept the charges! Dawn, is that really you?"

"Yes, Michael."

"My gosh, it's good to hear your voice."

Dawn blinked back tears. "Yours, too."

"Your letter arrived yesterday. I'd already heard about Montecristo. I'm awfully sorry."

"Thank you, but I think it was for the best."

"Why do you say that?"

"The place was never run properly. They were such idiots about—oh, never mind. That's not why I called. Listen, Michael, I've got something really important to talk to you about."

"Go ahead. I'm listening."

Dawn took a deep breath, then, shouting above the traffic, apologized for her behavior in Canada. She apologized for saying so little in her letter when she wanted to say more. Finally she got to the critical part. "I've been offered a fantastic job with the largest biological reserve in the country. The director is like Dr. Livingstone, a legend in his time."

"Sounds like a great opportunity," Michael said. "Are you going to take it?"

The connection was too poor and the traffic too loud for Dawn to pick up on the nuances in Michael's voice. She couldn't tell whether he was being conciliatory, sarcastic or indifferent. But to heck with pride. She would just have to take her chances. "I told Dr. Stratton I needed time to decide. That's why I phoned you. I would love to take the job, but I love you more, Michael. So I was wondering if your, uh . . . offer was still open."

"Which offer was that?"

Damn, he would have to make this difficult. "The one where I come to Canada and we share a life together— or whatever portion of our lives you see fit."

Michael, the dear man, didn't leave her dangling. He laughed gently and replied, "I was hoping that was the offer you meant, and the answer is yes. I still love you, more than ever, Dawn. So, please, come to Canada. I promise you'll never regret it."

13

Six months later Dawn was in Michael's kitchen inserting cloves into a ham. A blizzard was raging outdoors. The November storm had moved into Winnipeg the day before—a swirling mass of white that whipped and whistled around the balcony and through microscopic cracks in the window frames.

Michael was due to arrive from Vancouver at eight o'clock that evening. He was originally scheduled to come home the night before, but all flights had been canceled because of the weather.

Dawn couldn't believe how much she missed him. He had only been away three nights, but it felt like eternity. She couldn't bear the large empty bed without him—and judging from the phone calls she'd received, Michael felt the same way.

Logic told her that unless the blizzard stopped completely within the next two hours she'd be sleeping alone for the fourth night in a row. But Dawn stubbornly refused to entertain that possibility. She was going to bake this ham and toss a salad for Michael's dinner regardless. If she didn't do something to maintain her optimism, she'd end up climbing walls.

Dinner was ready on schedule. Michael wasn't. The dreaded phone call arrived while Dawn was whipping the meringue for a lemon pie.

"Hi, sweetie, it's me. Sorry it's taken me so long to call."

"That's okay. Where are you?"

"In Vancouver."

"Oh, no."

"Thanks to that prairie storm I won't make it home tonight, either."

Dawn resented the blinding whiteness outside, as though the snow had deliberately come between her and Michael. Still, she tried to sound cheerful. "I figured by now you wouldn't be. Is the weather all right there?"

"Raining, as usual. I hope you didn't bother making dinner or anything."

"Oh, no." Dawn stared disconsolately at the meringue. "Well, I did whip up a little something, but it wasn't any trouble."

"Good. How's the article coming?"

"Not great. I finished a rough draft today and read it over. It stinks."

"Come on, Dawn. You're being too hard on yourself."

"Are you kidding? I'm not being hard enough. Nobody would publish the drivel I'm writing."

For months Dawn had been working on a series of articles for scientific magazines on the importance of reforestation. She'd always considered herself disciplined, but not since she'd moved to Canada.

Dawn found it almost impossible to write while Michael was away. She would sit at her desk for hours, staring into space, missing him. Then she'd look at her computer screen, frustrated, and delete the whole thing.

With Michael around it was even harder to write. Except for weekends he was usually on the road three weeks out of four. Dawn couldn't bear to lock herself in the study on the rare occasions he was home.

She kept telling herself she would adjust, that eventually she would enjoy her time alone as she had in Costa Rica. But this wasn't Montecristo. When Michael was away, there was no jungle to wander through, no howler monkeys to keep her entertained. She didn't even feel like a scientist anymore—just a lonely grass widow who wrote for a hobby.

But enough of feeling sorry for herself. Michael must have felt just as lonely. "How did your training course go?" she asked brightly.

"It was terrific, but I'm exhausted. I can't wait to get home to you, baby."

"I can't wait, either. When do you think you can be here?"

"I'm booked on the first flight tomorrow morning. So why don't you fix yourself a nice hot bath and go to bed? With any luck you'll be woken up by a kiss."

Dawn laughed. "That sounds like the best offer I've heard in days. I love you, Michael."

"I love you, Dawn. Sweet dreams."

Her dreams were sweet, and as Michael promised, she was awakened with a kiss. In the middle of a gorgeous jungle setting Dawn felt moist, warm lips pressed to hers. She felt a tongue dipping into her mouth, nudging her gently, while strong hands cradled her face.

Still half asleep, she reached up and loosened his tie. Things were going to be fine for a while. Michael was home.

"I DON'T THINK I'm cut out to be a full-time writer," Dawn remarked that weekend while Michael prepared dinner.

He pulled two steaks out of the broiler and flipped them. "Why do you say that?"

"I can't seem to concentrate. I go stir-crazy stuck in that room every day."

He turned to her, his expression hurt. "Isn't the study comfortable?"

"Oh, yes, of course it is!" Dawn popped up from her chair to hug him. "I love the study. It makes me feel like a corporate president."

Heaven forbid, Michael should think she was ungrateful. No sooner had Dawn arrived in Canada than he'd spent countless evenings turning the spare bedroom into an office. He installed floor-to-ceiling shelves, suspended lighting and decorated the room with beautiful oak furniture. And if that wasn't enough, for their one-month anniversary he presented Dawn with a state-of-the-art, laptop computer. She spent the next three months battling the one-eyed monster and watching it devour her efforts. A typewriter would have been easier, but she never had the heart to tell him.

"Maybe you should work on something else," he suggested, playing with a curl close to her ear. "Set those articles aside for a while."

"I tried that. It doesn't work." She leaned into his hand, rubbing her cheek against the wiry hair of his knuckles. "I think I need to get out more. Not to restaurants or anything. Just outside."

"What's stopping you?"

"Three feet of snow."

Michael's jaw pulsed. "Right. I forgot."

"But I did go for a walk in the park yesterday," Dawn said, trying quickly to lighten the mood. "It was lovely."

"But it's not the tropics."

"Well, no."

Winter had descended early, even for Manitoba. The first snowfall had arrived in September and, except for the occasional brief thaw, had remained on the ground. Dawn had enjoyed the novelty of winter until the first time she'd tried driving in it. While approaching an intersection she'd applied her brakes too quickly, hit a patch of ice and skidded into oncoming traffic. Fortunately everyone else in Winnipeg had seemed to know what they were doing, so Dawn was spared. But she'd come away from the incident shaken and even more homesick for the snowless mountain roads of Costa Rica. She had a sense Michael knew it, too.

The steaks were ready. He took them out of the oven and laid them on wooden platters. Dawn tossed the salad and poured two glasses of burgundy.

"Look, Dawn," he said after they'd eaten in silence for a few minutes. "I know you don't like cold weather, and I wish there was something I could do about it."

She managed a brave smile. "But you can't, so why worry?"

"I can't help it. Every time I go away I'm afraid I'll come home to an empty house and a Dear John letter."

"I would never do anything like that." She reached across the table for his hand. "I love you, Michael."

"I know you love me. And I love you. But I feel so helpless knowing that you're feeling cooped up while I'm away. That's no life for you."

"I'm adjusting. Really I am."

Michael stared at her a minute, then lowered his gaze and silently refilled their glasses.

It bothered Dawn to realize how easily Michael could read her thoughts. Not that she was hiding anything. She did love him dearly, and it amazed her how compatible they were.

When he was home, which wasn't often, there was scarcely a harsh word between them. They made love every night and most mornings, too. He phoned her from the office at least once a day and was constantly surprising her with gifts. Last week it was a huge tropical plant. This week leather gloves to match her new winter coat. Dawn had never felt so pampered in her life—nor so useless.

"I've been toying with an idea," she said, "about what I could do instead of writing articles, but it might take some time to put together."

Michael's face brightened. "I love ideas. Let me hear it."

Dawn proceeded cautiously at first until she remembered she had nothing to fear from her lover. He was such a strong man, so secure in himself that he never found it necessary to belittle anyone. She'd never met a man who was so consistently supportive. At times, she still had to remind herself he was real.

"I've received a few letters from colleagues in the States," she said, "inviting me to present a lecture on rain forest management to graduate students."

"That's fantastic, Dawn. Where would you lecture?"

"One of the offers is from Berkeley, another is a college in New England. But that's just the tip of the iceberg." She laughed and shivered. "Pardon the frigid analogy. Apparently there's enough interest in global ecology these days that I could develop a full-time lecture circuit across North America. Not just to students, but I could also raise funds with social service groups."

"You could end up traveling as much as I do, and there's good money in it, too."

Dawn nodded. "Almost embarrassingly so."

"You're an expert in your field," Michael pointed out. "Don't be modest about claiming your worth."

"I'm trying not to be," she said, but it still wasn't sitting well. After asking around, Dawn discovered that with her qualifications she could command a fee of several thousand dollars for a one-hour speech. At first she was appalled at the sum. In Montecristo she had earned as much in six months—if the money came in at all. But if that was what people were paying to be enlightened for an hour, who was she to complain?

"I was hoping that if things worked out," she continued, "we could synchronize our traveling. I could schedule my lectures around your loss control audits, so we wouldn't have to be apart so often."

"That's a beautiful idea!"

"You wouldn't be distracted if I traveled with you?"

Michael's gaze skimmed her body lovingly. "I'd be distracted out of my mind, but I'd love it. You have got to know, honey, that I don't like being alone in hotel rooms at night. I want you with me every chance I can get."

Dawn grinned. "Oh, good. I was hoping you'd say that."

FIVE MONTHS LATER Dawn was speaking to the Houston Horticultural Society when Michael stepped into the banquet hall. He'd just finished an audit with a major restaurant chain and was hoping he would get away soon enough to catch Dawn's speech. But he could tell from the context that she was nearly finished. Oh, well, he thought, her finales were always the best part, anyway.

He looked around the room. Several hundred guests, decked out in their finest, had paid an exorbitant sum for creamed chicken and the opportunity to hear Dawn lecture. She was doing a great job, too. A hush had fallen across the room, and every head—including Michael's now—was turned to the podium.

"I wish I could have brought the forest with me," Dawn was saying, gesturing with the same grace that had blown him away in Costa Rica. "I wish you could smell the orchids for yourself, feel the texture of the trees they feed on. There's a sound that's peculiar to the rain forest, a subliminal hum that, once you've heard it, you never forget. To me, that sound represents life itself, a confirmation of our coexistence with nature. But let me assure you, ladies and gentlemen, as species die off and land erodes, that hum grows fainter by the minute. Let's not, in our complacency, allow the forests to fall silent—or there will be no one left to hear the sound...not even us."

The applause was thunderous. Michael couldn't have been prouder as Dawn stepped off the dais to greet a throng of admirers. She was going to be exhausted, as usual, once the adrenaline wore off. They had been traveling together for three months, so he knew how the routine hit her. But this latest two-week stint was worse than most. Three seminars and six audits for Michael and as many lectures for Dawn. They had traveled from Washington to Texas and there was still another engagement in Detroit.

Michael was delighted to have Dawn with him, and she thrived on the opportunity to educate the public. It was not, however, the idyllic situation he had hoped it would be. There were just too many technicalities. Flight schedules, car rentals, hotel bookings—and people.

After years of experience, Michael had learned how to fend off clients who wanted to wine and dine him until the wee hours. Dawn was still grappling with that one. More often than not, she'd get cornered by some overbearing society matron, and she and Michael would end up smearing caviar on toast for the evening instead of making love. It wasn't good for his waistline—and murder on his libido. He was going to have to explain things to her soon.

"There you are, honey," Dawn said. "I was hoping you'd get away in time to meet me."

She put her arms around Michael and kissed him warmly on the mouth. Michael returned her exuberance. That was one thing he had to say about Dawn. She didn't believe in pecks, those pitiful excuses for affection that people resorted to in public. He felt proud to love her and saw no reason to hide the fact.

"I only caught the last few minutes," he said, "but you were fabulous."

"Do you think so?"

"You're getting better all the time."

"Thanks. That means a lot, coming from you." She linked an arm around his and steered him toward an ominous-looking group of socialites.

"Where are we going?" he asked.

"There are some people we have to meet."

Michael slowed down deliberately. "Why do we have to meet them?"

Dawn sighed. "Because they wield a lot of influence and have more money than they know what to do with."

Maybe they didn't have to have that talk. Maybe Dawn was catching on to things herself.

"Okay," he replied cautiously, "but no cocktail parties, okay?"

"None. I promise."

Michael hadn't noticed until now, but the lines at the corners of Dawn's eyes were deeper than usual. So were the shadows beneath them. He remembered in Costa

Rica when she never wore makeup, never needed to. Dawn always looked healthy and bronzed and totally natural. But these days she was pale and had to resort to cosmetics in public. In Michael's estimation Dawn was still beautiful, but it was a strained kind of beauty that made him feel sad.

They got off lucky with the matrons. Dawn introduced him to the mayor of the city and several of her wealthy constituents, but they didn't proffer the usual invitation of cocktails and hors d'oeuvres.

"You must be exhausted after all that touring," one buxom woman said to Dawn with a wink. "You just take that gorgeous man to your hotel room and relax."

Dawn grinned proudly at Michael. "I intend to."

She was thanked for her efforts, congratulated and promised a sizable check toward the Reforestation Fund of Costa Rica.

Dawn looked as relieved as Michael felt when they finally reached their room. The first thing she did was kick off her shoes. Then she flopped backward onto the bed. "That's it. I've had it. I don't care if I ever see another podium in my life."

"You poor baby. Roll over and let me give you a backrub."

"Oh, would you? I'd love you forever."

"All the more reason." Michael felt drained, as well, but after years of traveling he had learned how to pace his energy. Dawn still tended to burn hers in one massive fireball.

He tossed aside his suit coat, rolled up his sleeves and climbed onto the bed above Dawn's head. First he ran his fingers through her hair. No pressure, just a light, rhythmic combing of his skin against her scalp.

"Oh, that feels wonderful," Dawn said, shutting her eyes blissfully.

"It's supposed to." Michael lowered his head briefly to kiss her neck, then intensified the movement of his fingers. Finally he pressed both palms flat against the top of her skull and held them there, allowing his own energy to channel through and invigorate.

It was a relaxation technique he had read somewhere called craniopathy. How it worked, he didn't know. But it did work—especially on Dawn. He soon had her smiling and moaning softly on the bed, forgetting the reasons for her stress.

"Do you have to see any clients tonight?" she asked, reaching up to skim her hands along his chest.

"Nope."

Still lying on her back, Dawn began to undo his shirt buttons, starting from the top. "You mean we really have the whole evening to ourselves?"

"The whole evening." The lower she got, the shallower his breath. When she reached Michael's belt, she tugged the shirt out and rasped her hand, none too innocently, against his groin. "Good grief, woman, it's a good thing we don't have anywhere to go tonight. I have a feeling we'd be late."

Deftly she rolled over and sat up on her knees. They were now face-to-face on the bed, gazing at each other with a hunger that usually came with prolonged deprivation.

"When's the last time we spent all evening making love?" Dawn asked, raining kisses along his stubbled chin.

"I'm not sure. It was either Oregon or Nevada."

"Oregon," she mumbled, drawing his earlobe gently into her mouth. "I fell asleep in Nevada."

"That's right, too. You were so tired."

"But I'm not tired now."

"So I've noticed."

She placed her hands on his shoulders, and they both tipped over onto the bed. Michael slid his hands beneath Dawn's high-necked cashmere sweater and fingered the lace on her bra. She didn't care for bras, but depending on her attire, they were a requirement in her present occupation. Michael knew she wasn't crazy about dressing up every day, either, but she'd learned to accept that, as well. He was impressed with Dawn's adaptability. She really did make a fine companion—both in bed and out.

As he lifted her sweater and unclasped her bra, a rush of memories flooded through him. It astonished him to realize that nearly a year had passed since they'd met. A year of loving the same woman.

He was still waiting, however, for Dawn to adjust to his life-style, as though she had just arrived. Now he wasn't so sure she could. He knew that she was loyal, determined to please and very much in love. But she was still missing something, a magic ingredient that Michael suspected could only be found in one part of the world.

"Where are you, Michael?" Dawn teased. She had unzipped his pants, and her hands were tucked into his briefs. She was obviously waiting for him to lift his hips.

The want in her eyes refueled Michael's hope. Dawn looked tired, but every bit as aroused as she'd been during their first months together.

Maybe things weren't as bad as he thought. Maybe he was wrong to compare this exhausted lecturer to the free-spirited Dawn from Costa Rica. Sure, their lives were a little more complicated than he would have liked, but their love was as strong as ever. That was enough to make a relationship work, wasn't it? *Wasn't it?* The question remained unanswered as Michael removed the last of his lover's clothes and lowered himself over her.

DAWN ENTERED the apartment first, shivering as she crossed the hall and turned up the thermostat. Then she noticed something out of the corner of her eye. "Oh, doh, Michael," she said through her nose. "My plant's dead!"

Sure enough, the dracaena he'd bought to remind Dawn of the jungle was brown and withered. Sniffling, she bent down in front of the brittle stalk. Michael wasn't sure, but he didn't think Dawn was crying. It was just that darn cold she'd caught in Detroit. Poor thing, she'd been running a fever and talking nasally for two days.

He came up from behind and hugged her. "I'll get you a new one, honey. I promise."

She turned and looked up at him through bleary eyes. "Doh, Michael, you don't have to. We travel too much to look after plants."

"Maybe you're right. But I do know one thing for sure. If you're ever going to get rid of that cold, you have to rest. I'll make some hot tea and honey and bring it to you in bed."

Dawn felt too miserable to argue. She just laid her head on his shoulder. "You're so good to me. I'm sorry I got sick and ruined the rest of our trip."

"Don't be silly. You didn't ruin anything."

Michael told himself it was too soon to start worrying. The surprise trip he'd planned to Costa Rica was still a month away. Dawn would have plenty of time to recover by then.

AS IT TURNED OUT, a month wasn't enough. Dawn's cold lodged in her chest, then turned into a severe case of bronchitis. She spent virtually the entire month in bed, coughing and feverish. She was forced to cancel two speaking engagements and stay home while Michael traveled to Montreal and Boston.

It was the worst month of Dawn's life. Her lungs were in constant agony, and the coughing never let up, night or day. Michael postponed most of his local appointments so that he could stay home and look after her, but in a way, Dawn wished he wouldn't.

Seeing him so worried tore her apart, and he wasn't getting the rest he needed. Dawn wanted him to sleep in the spare room so that her coughing wouldn't disturb him, but Michael wouldn't hear of it.

She felt even worse that their sex life was nonexistent, but there was no way she could have accommodated him. Still, every night, Michael insisted on holding Dawn until she fell asleep, exhausted, in his arms. It was almost as though he held himself responsible for her illness, though why he should feel that way, Dawn couldn't imagine.

One morning when she had enough strength to eat in the kitchen, Dawn tried to absolve him of his guilt. "Remember when I told you about living in North Dakota? I was sick all the time then, too."

"But you were just a kid."

"It doesn't matter. Cold weather still affects me this way."

Lines of fatigue were etched deep into Michael's face. He looked at least ten years older than before she got sick. "I guess I never should have asked you to move here."

Dawn's mouth dropped. "Michael, what are you saying?"

"Oh, honey, don't get me wrong. I love you. I can't imagine living without you anymore, but . . ."

"But what?"

He took both her hands in his. "I've watched you this past year, Dawn. You've tried so hard to adjust, and you've loved me so beautifully, but you can't really be yourself when you're away from the tropics, can you?"

Dawn's eyes widened. She wasn't sure whether to panic or be grateful for Michael's perception. "Is it that obvious?"

"To me, it is. And only when I forced myself to look. I've made some major blunders, Dawn. First I treated you like a hothouse flower, and that didn't work. Then I agreed to let you travel with me, and you're not cut out for life on the road, either—especially not during the cold months."

"That doesn't say much for my stamina, does it?"

"Are you kidding? You're one of the strongest women I know. You used to haul your own water every day, remember? You took me on a hike through Montecristo that would have killed most mortal men, and you weren't even breathing hard."

Shoulders slumped, she covered her mouth to prevent another coughing fit. "Maybe so, but look at me now. I can barely make it to the bedroom on my own steam."

"That's only because you're ill. But I'm going to make you well again, I promise. And then we're going to take a long, hard look at what we want out of life."

"But I want you, Michael. Nothing more."

"And I want you, Dawn . . . forever. That's why I'm going to make sure we don't screw it up."

DAWN WAS DEVASTATED when she learned that Michael was going to Costa Rica, and she couldn't go. It was to have been a business and pleasure trip combined. But

Dawn's doctor was adamant. She wouldn't be well enough to travel for at least another month. Meanwhile, Michael was unable to postpone his visit to Agrofin.

He promised to phone her every day, and he took a list of things to bring back for Dawn. A week's worth of San José newspapers, the latest gossip from Lito and her favorite coconut candy. Dawn had no way of knowing, but with any luck Michael was going to bring her a lot more than that.

As usual he'd done his homework ahead of time. Michael knew exactly who to contact and what approach to use concerning Montecristo. The board was dissolved, but the land didn't go up for sale as Dawn had originally feared. The Costa Rican government, recognizing the importance of rain forests, was holding the acreage in abeyance. All they wanted was someone to offer them a solution.

Michael completed his two-day audit of Agrofin, then drove to San José where he met first with government officials, then with Carlomagno, Agrofin's chief executive officer. The young scion was delighted with Michael's work. Thanks to his loss control system, the grain producing company was now accident-free and reaping a profit.

Carlomagno, meanwhile, had proven his worth to the family. Michael had earned the man's loyalty. Now the time had come to put it to a test.

They met for dinner in San José's swank Gran Hotel. Carlomagno pulled his usual number—ordering the most expensive, not necessarily the best, items on the menu. Michael didn't mind. Having worked with the man, he knew Carlomagno's ostentation was not so much arrogance as a mark of insecurity. That boded well for both of them. Carlomagno would be predisposed to listen, while Michael could offer something that would raise the young man's esteem even higher in his family's eyes.

"I understand your family is actively involved in charities and philanthropic causes," Michael began while his client snipped off the tip of a cigar.

"Oh, yes. My mother supports the opera, and my father is active with the National Museum."

"What about you, Carlomagno? Have you ever considered investing in your own worthwhile cause?"

"I am approached constantly by charities and associations. If I responded to all of them, my assets would be depleted within the year."

"I'm not talking about doling out millions of colones. I'm talking about donating time, as chairman of a board of directors."

Carlomagno's cheeks reddened. "At my age?"

Michael nodded.

"I'm not sure. I have never even considered . . ."

"I can promise you it won't be a losing proposition. I'll do loss control free of charge, and I can provide you with an excellent recommendation for staffing."

The young man set down his cigar and leaned across the table. "It sounds fascinating. What would I be heading?"

"You would be chairman of Costa Rica's second largest biological reserve—Montecristo."

DAWN HAD PACED her energy carefully so that she wouldn't be exhausted when Michael came home. She wanted to prepare something special for dinner and decided on an Indonesian feast, full of finger foods and exotic spices—guaranteed to seduce even the weariest of palates. Many of the dishes could be prepared ahead of time, so she was able to alternate cooking and resting.

Several hours before Michael's arrival Dawn took a long, hot bath and pampered her body deliciously. She had to be getting better. For the first time in weeks her sex drive was back. And it was back with a vengeance. She hoped Michael hadn't given up on her yet—knowing deep in her heart that he never would.

The door opened right on cue, and Dawn was ready. She stepped into the entryway and smiled. "Welcome home, darling."

Michael's eyes popped. "Holy jumping, do you look fabulous."

"Thank you."

She was wearing her emerald silk blouse, with the top three buttons seductively undone, and a slim-fitting black skirt with a slit up the side. Her dark, glossy curls were loose and fell heavily to her shoulders. Every detail from Dawn's high-heeled pumps to the touch of perfume at her wrists was designed to drive her man wild.

As soon as he took her into his arms, Dawn knew she had succeeded. "Oh, baby, you're feeling better," he said. "I'm so glad."

"I am, thanks to your wonderful bedside manner."

Michael took his time kissing her, not even bothering to take off his coat. He kissed Dawn's eyelids, her nose and the tip of her chin. He feasted on her curves and reveled in her touch. From all indications it was going to be a beautiful night.

He loved the *rijstaffel*, and that delighted Dawn. They lingered over dinner for hours, while Michael provided her with tidbits from Costa Rica. She devoured every last detail from the weather to the crop reports. Then, quite by accident, she led them to the topic Michael had been saving for the end.

"What about Montecristo? Have you heard anything about it?"

"As a matter of fact, I have." He topped off her cappuccino, then pulled a sheaf of documents from the briefcase he'd left nearby. "Looks like it might be reopened as a biological reserve."

He watched Dawn's reaction carefully and was pleased with what he saw. There was delight on her face, relief and just a touch of envy.

"Really?" she said.

"The government is in the process of assigning a new board of directors who will be looking at the staffing. If all goes well, they might reopen in a few months."

"Oh." Dawn folded her hands on the table, but Michael noticed they were shaking. "I wonder who they have in mind for staff."

Michael found it interesting that Dawn hadn't questioned how he knew all these things. She was obviously too intrigued with the topic. "They plan to use as many of the former employees as they can. In fact, I have a letter here from the minister of natural resources to that effect."

Michael handed her an envelope. Dawn tore it open and scanned the letter's contents. Her eyes widened. "They're offering me the position of Montecristo's director!"

"No kidding?"

She looked up, perplexed, confused and more excited than he'd seen her in months. "You knew all this. But how could you know?"

"Connections."

Now she looked horrified. "You didn't pull strings or anything . . ."

"I did nothing except plant a few bugs in the right ears. The rest is up to you, Dawn."

"But I can't accept this. You and I are . . ." The words for what they actually were escaped her.

"We're lovers," Michael offered, "and I'm hoping we'll be a lot more than that soon."

Dawn let the paper flutter to the table. "Would you please explain to me what's going on? You're looking at me as though you expect me to take the job at Montecristo."

"Don't you want to?"

"I'd love nothing better, but I love you, Michael. I don't want us to go back to what we were before."

Michael reached into another suit coat pocket and brought out a small velvet box. "Neither do I. That's why I was hoping you might consider being my wife instead of just my lover."

Dawn opened the box and found a flawless solitaire diamond. "Oh, my gosh . . ."

"Would you consider marrying me, Dawn—even if you became the director of Montecristo?"

"Yes, but . . . of course I'd marry you. My goodness. But where would we live? How would we . . ." She ran a hand across her face, knowing the flush on her cheeks had little to do with residual fever.

"I'm going to juggle my schedule," Michael said, "so I only have to work seven months of the year. The rest of the time I can be with you. As for setting up Montecristo, I can help with personnel planning so that you'll be free to leave the reserve at least three months of the year. That will give us eight months together out of twelve."

Dawn tried to compute in her head. "Okay, let me figure out what you're saying. Right now you're traveling, what . . . three weeks out of four?"

"Yes. That means we're either apart seventy-five percent of the year or on the road, wearing ourselves out. Which sounds better to you?"

"Eight months out of twelve together, definitely." Dawn stared at the ring again, then looked up at Michael. "You would actually allow me to return to Montecristo, and we would be . . ." She couldn't quite get the word out. *Married?*

"Married," he said for her. "And another thing, Dawn. Allowing you to take the job doesn't even enter the picture. I'm not into ownership. I only want to keep my woman happy and love her the best way I know how."

"By letting me return to Costa Rica."

Michael took her hands across the table. "Costa Rica is your world. I should have understood that sooner, but I do now."

"Are you sure we'll have eight months together?"

"Every year until I retire. Then you might be stuck with me year-round."

Dawn shook her head. "I can't believe it. It will be like sharing the best of everything."

"That's what I want to do, honey."

She looked at him again, eyes shimmering with promise. "I want the same, Michael. To share my world, your world . . . the best of both."

HARLEQUIN Temptation

Lovers Apart

FOUR CONTROVERSIAL STORIES! FOUR DYNAMITE AUTHORS!

In this new Temptation miniseries, four modern couples are separated by jobs, distance or emotional barriers and must work to find a resolution.

Don't miss the LOVERS APART miniseries—four special Temptation books—one per month beginning in January 1991. Look for...

January: Title #332
DIFFERENT WORLDS by Elaine K. Stirling
Dawn and Michael . . . A brief passionate affair left them aching for more, but a continent stood between them.

February: Title #336
DÉTENTE by Emma Jane Spenser
Kassidy and Matt . . . Divorce was the solution to their battles—but it didn't stop the fireworks in the bedroom!

March: Title #340
MAKING IT by Elise Title
Hannah and Marc . . . Can a newlywed yuppie couple—both partners having demanding careers—find ''time'' for love?

April: Title #344
YOUR PLACE OR MINE by Vicki Lewis Thompson
Lila and Bill . . . A divorcée and a widower share a shipboard romance but they're too set in their ways to survive on land!

LAP-1

Coming soon
to an easy chair near you.

FIRST CLASS is Harlequin's armchair travel plan for the incurably romantic. You'll visit a different dreamy destination every month from January through December without ever packing a bag. No jet lag, no expensive air fares and *no* lost luggage. Just First Class Harlequin Romance reading, featuring exotic settings from Tasmania to Thailand, from Egypt to Australia, and more.

FIRST CLASS romantic excursions guaranteed! Start your world tour in January. Look for the special **FIRST CLASS** destination on selected Harlequin Romance titles—there's a new one every month.

NEXT DESTINATION:
THAILAND

 Harlequin Books

JTR2

COMING IN 1991 FROM
HARLEQUIN SUPERROMANCE:

Three abandoned orphans,
one missing heiress!

Dying millionaire Owen Byrnside receives an
anonymous letter informing him that twenty-six years
ago, his son, Christopher, fathered a daughter. The
infant was abandoned at a foundling home that
subsequently burned to the ground, destroying all
records. Three young women could be Owen's long-
lost granddaughter, and Owen is determined to track
down each of them! Read their stories in

#434 HIGH STAKES (available January 1991)
#438 DARK WATERS (available February 1991)
#442 BRIGHT SECRETS (available March 1991)

Three exciting stories of intrigue and romance by
veteran Superromance author Jane Silverwood.

You'll flip . . . your pages won't!
Read paperbacks *hands-free* with

Book Mate ·I

The perfect "mate" for all your romance paperbacks

Traveling • Vacationing • At Work • In Bed • Studying • Cooking • Eating

Perfect size for all standard paperbacks, this wonderful invention makes reading a pure pleasure! Ingenious design holds paperback books OPEN and FLAT so even wind can't ruffle pages— leaves your hands free to do other things. Reinforced, wipe-clean vinyl-covered holder flexes to let you turn pages without undoing the strap . . . supports paperbacks so well, they have the strength of hardcovers!

Pages turn WITHOUT opening the strap

SEE-THROUGH STRAP

Reinforced back stays flat

Built in bookmark

BOOK MARK

BACK COVER HOLDING STRIP

10˝ x 7¼˝ opened.
Snaps closed for easy carrying, too